✠   ✠   ✠   ✠   ✠

CHARLOTTE VALE ALLEN

MIXED EMOTIONS

Island Nation Press LLC

✦ 144 ROWAYTON WOODS DRIVE ✦ NORWALK, CT ✦ 06854 ✦

✠ ✠ ✠ ✠ ✠

Mixed Emotions

ISBN 0-9657437-8-0

First Published in the USA
by Warner Books 1977

This edition published by
Island Nation Press LLC 1998

Cover & book design by deLancey Funsten.

Island Nation Books LLC
144 Rowayton Woods Drive
Norwalk, CT 06854

Printed in the United States

✠ ✠ ✠ ✠ ✠

Visit the author's website at:
http://www.charlottevaleallen.com

MIXED EMOTIONS

✠   ✠   ✠   ✠   ✠

One

THEY MET AT A PARTY. PAUL CAME WITH ANOTHER GIRL but spent so much time staring at Margot that his date became angry, threatening to walk out on him if he didn't stop. He tried to tear his attention away from Margot but he simply couldn't.

She wasn't the best-looking girl he'd ever seen. She had a dainty, heart-shaped face with an appealing, upturning mouth and prominent cheekbones. But her eyes, he thought, were really fantastic. Big, wide-set, hazel. Eyes that flashed with life, with amusement, with a kind of excitement. She seemed to be constantly moving even when she wasn't. He couldn't stop watching her, she seemed so totally alive. His eyes returned again and again to observe how her head tilted back when she laughed, how her eyes seemed to glow and get bigger when she talked. He considered ways of approaching her, things he might say. He had to meet her, find out if she was as good as she looked.

Having him watching her was a little embarrassing, but exciting. Something that had never happened to Margot before. She'd had boys come marching up to her with remarks they'd obviously carefully prepared, but she'd never been the object of such an intense visual study.

Maybe he was staring because there was something wrong

with her, something she hadn't noticed. A strap showing, her slip hanging down. Or a button undone. She discreetly checked her clothing, then became impatient. With herself. With him. She wished he'd stop. There was nothing wrong with her. But his staring made her feel there was.

As the party progressed, she became more and more acutely aware of his eyes following her until there was no excitement left, only the embarrassment. If I was that girl, she thought, glancing at his date, I'd be furious. And hurt. I'd feel so terrible. She was glad not to be that girl, but felt a little sorry for her.

She was rescued by Roy, the brother of the girl who was giving the party. She turned away to talk to him, making herself listen closely to what he was saying. She helped herself to a sandwich and some potato salad and continued chatting with Roy, wishing, as she often did, she could be in love with him. He was very good-looking, very intelligent, very open-minded, very kind. Very everything, it seemed. But the few times they'd dated had been nothing more than fraternally pleasant. His end-of-the-evening kisses and tentative caresses left her feeling empty, unaffected. You couldn't force feeling where none existed. It was too bad because Roy was someone she believed it'd be easy to live with, get through time with.

Somebody stacked records on the turntable and dancing started. It was a good party. Suzanne's parties always were. She laid on a lot of food, coerced each of the guys into bringing a bottle, then got out of the way and let things happen. She didn't bother with hostessy efforts like introductions and fussy arrays of food. She just got everything and everyone together, then moved into the middle of the action and enjoyed whatever evolved.

Margot danced. She loved dancing, loved knowing she was graceful and completely uninhibited in her movements. She loved the flow, the rhythm, the freedom. She danced when leaving movie theaters, danced alone in her room to the radio, danced at a party with anyone who asked. She'd been nicknamed Sunny in high school and liked that. She felt happy. She was twenty-one, in her senior year at the City University and, for the most part, unconcerned about the future. She had no idea what she'd do after this year but felt sure something would come along. Something would. So there wasn't much point worrying about it the way a number of her friends did. She was having too much fun to worry about careers or the future.

Her mother encouraged her to be relaxed about her future. "In time, the future will come to you. There is no point in hurrying to it."

Her mother gave her one of her infrequent smiles that were like rewards. As a small child, Margot had worked for those smiles, doing things she believed would win them for her. Her mother was serious, very clever—Margot had sensed this without ever being told—and very realistic. Listening to conversations between her parents, Margot had at various times heard her mother say, "I grow so tired of the people who constantly complain of their problems. In that sense, I have no problems." And, "Perhaps I was too unaware, or disinterested, but my childhood and adolescence were happy times. There were problems but I didn't see them. Only later could I see. And by then, it was as if I had become insulated. There was an amazing perspective to what I saw."

Periodic remarks like these led Margot into quiet corners to think. The things her mother said seemed to require thought. Margot concluded her mother was, in some indefinable fashion, attempting to make Margot's childhood as happy as she remembered her own to be.

Her father volunteered money for her education, occasional unexpected bear hugs and a placid acceptance of his daughter's exuberance and his wife's clear-eyed evaluations of life around them. There were times when he wondered how Margot could be so aware academically yet so blithely gay in the face of life's realities.

Margot considered him to be a pessimist, and had once spent a season attempting to force a more optimistic outlook upon him. He resisted gently, saying, "We are not all blessed, chére Margot, with eyes such as yours. Not all of us are able to see so much good in people as you would see in them. You must learn it is not possible to force people to look with your eyes. You cannot make changes by force."

She loved them both. When she listened to the complaints of her friends about their families, she wondered why they couldn't simply accept their parents as being people; why they couldn't take what was being offered and stop expecting more; stop being so overcritical. But Papa was right. You couldn't force people to see. So she taught herself to stop trying.

There were moments when she felt frightened, apprehensive about the future. Because the future was such a vast, indefinite place that seemed to stretch into infinity; it seemed it would take an enormous amount of concentration and effort to work your way inch by inch toward it. When the doubts came, she faced them down or danced them out of her system. Her life would solve itself eventually.

She knew her father thought her a little too lighthearted. She wasn't. She simply believed it was easier being pleasant.

Roy went out to the kitchen to get more beer. Margot noticed with relief that the "starer" and his date seemed to have left. She went upstairs to the bathroom to splash water on her face and neck, cool herself down. When she returned, Roy handed her a bottle of beer, then went to change the records. She was standing by the window drinking the beer, hating the taste of it, when the "starer" came back. As she watched him make his way toward her, she was suddenly nervous. It was a rare, unpleasant sensation. Few people made her really nervous, but this man did. Something was about to happen; something different, something serious. She had no idea how to handle this situation and it worried her.

The "starer" leaned against the wall beside her and lit a cigarette, saying, "Pretend like you don't know me, Louis. Make like you ain't never seen me before. Don't look! Just keep on looking over there like you was, Louis. I got a message for ya from the chief."

She burst out laughing and looked at him wide-eyed.

"Are you nuts?" she laughed. "What's *that*?"

He glanced around straight-faced. "Jeez! Did I *tell* ya, Louis! You wanna blow this whole thing? The chief wants ta see ya. He's got a job for ya. You're the only one's got the right kinda fingers for this kinda safe, see." He took hold of her hand and studied her fingertips. "Aw, jeez, Louis! Didn't I tell you to keep on sanding down them tips?"

She laughed harder and he smiled, folding his hand around hers. He was nice-looking. Sandy brown hair, blue eyes. A cheeky, mischievous face. She was slightly taller than he. Which made him about five-seven. Of course, without her shoes ... What difference does that make? she asked herself impatiently.

"Dance?" he asked, smiling, his eyes on her like an intimate caress.

"Okay." She smiled back. He took her bottle, dropped his cigarette into it, set the bottle down on the window sill and fitted her into his arms.

"Say, Louis!" He laughed softly, directing her here, here, moving her over the floor. "You're a female, Louis! How come ya never clued me?"

"You're really out of your mind!" she said, smiling into his face, experiencing a breathless, sinking sensation. Excited. "Is this your usual routine?"

"Quiet!" he whispered, letting his eyes suspiciously rove over the faces of people nearby. "Everyone's a spy. D'ya see that mike in the beer bottle? Killed it with my cigarette. Lucky thing for you, Louis. Ya gotta keep your eyes peeled every minute. Never know when they'll get the drop onya."

Her sides were beginning to ache from laughing.

"What's your real name, Louis?" he asked softly into her ear so that his voice seemed to echo inside her skull. She could feel his breath on her cheek, in her hair.

"Margot Seaton. What's yours?" She looked into his eyes feeling suddenly wonderfully happy, high.

"Don't give it away, see! I'm Paul. Code name. Rayburn. I've got an escape route planned outta this joint. Soon's this number's wound down, grab your stuff and I'll get you out. We've got forty minutes to make that boat to Calais. They're watching all the terminals. It's our only chance."

She couldn't stop laughing, smiling. They looked at each other for several moments and she felt everything inside her expanding receptively.

"Great dancer, Lou!" he said. "Just great!"

"You're not bad yourself, fella." She was swinging easily into this game. "For a crook."

He hugged her and laughed delightedly. "I knew you were the one," he said, his right hand low on her spine. "Knew it the minute I saw you. You're not too old for me, are ya, Louis?"

"I don't know. I'll be twenty-two in April."

"Thank God!" He sighed dramatically. "I got closeta six years on ya. It's gonna be okay."

"That's lucky," she said, making a sober face. "I'm not ready yet for that older-woman stuff."

"You wanna get married tonight or wait 'til next Thursday?"

She laughed. "What's next Thursday?"

"Only free afternoon," he said, maneuvering her between

two chairs and out into the hallway.

"I see." Her face was flooded with heat, color. "And I've got to make up my mind fast. Right?" She was drowning beneath her clothes.

"You got it!" He smiled again and she looked at his mouth. She dared look at his teeth, his soft-looking lips. His face seemed to be changing before her eyes, becoming familiar, becoming important. "Live at home with the folks, Louis?"

"That's right. It's a good cover."

"Smart! Very, very smart."

"I thought so."

"I'm nuts about your eyes," he said, then quickly, managing to look furtive, glanced around. "Quick!" he whispered urgently. "This is it! Grab your gear and let's make it out!"

Smiling giddily, she grabbed her coat and bag and they hurried out. Their laughter seemed to ring in the deserted street. He took her arm, looked up, then down the street, then said, "Now!" and started running with her, pulling her to a stop in front of a white Thunderbird. He unlocked the door, she quickly climbed in as he raced around to the other side, arriving just as she dived across the seat to unlock the door.

"Great!" He laughed, fitting the key into the ignition. "You always was a great getaway man, Louis!"

They pulled away fast from the curb as he asked, "Hungry?"

"I've already eaten. At the party," she said, studying his profile. She liked his face, liked the bright color riding in his cheeks. He looked so good, so happy.

"Okay," he said, "we'll cruise a little."

She sat back, enjoying herself; her chest feeling strained, overfull of laughter, anticipation. She thought perhaps she'd always wanted somebody to come along and create excitement this way.

"What do they call you?" he asked, fiddling with the dials on the radio.

"What do they call *you*?" she countered, finding it natural to fence words with him.

"What do they call me?" He looked over at her. "Paul. What else?"

"Unimaginative. They call *me* Sunny."

"Oh, now that's *highly* imaginative," he said. "Wonderfully original, clever."

"And you could do better," she challenged.

"Anybody could. Let's see. I've got to be able to come up with the absolutely perfect, simply adorable nickname. There must be a million. Muffy. Buffy. Fippy. Tippy."

She laughed. "God! They're pretty awful, aren't they? Call me Margot. I'd be embarrassed now being called Sunny."

"See! Told you I'd come up with the perfect name. Now," he said, "come on over here a little closer and tell me about Margot. You at school? Or do you work?"

"I'm a senior."

"Doing what?"

"Fine Arts."

"Which interests you?" he asked, lighting another cigarette, offering her one, which she refused.

"It's your turn. What do you do?"

"Me?" He laughed. She liked the sound of it better and better. "I am what is known as your junior executive."

"Impressive. Doing what, junior?"

"Pushing around a lot of paper right now. Eventually, I'm supposed to get right down into it and push people around." He laughed again. "Not literally, naturally. Management."

"What sort of company?"

"Ah!" he sighed. "There's your proverbial fly in the ointment. Investment banking. All that beautiful money and none for me to play with."

"You're not exactly starving from the looks of it."

"True. Anyway, how about Saturday night? Dinner? You're the best with the footwork, Louis. We could do a little tripping of the old light fantastic. 'Course I don't know how I'll make it through an entire week without seeing you."

This is where I'm supposed to play hard to get, she thought, not show I'm too eager; lie about another date, stall him, force him to call a couple of times.

"Saturday's too far away," she said, a helpless smile taking shape on her mouth.

"I knew it!" he declared, reaching out to put his arm across her shoulders. "I just *knew!*"

"What did you know?" she asked softly, overwhelmed.

"That I'd fall for a girl with big flashing eyes and all kinds of rhythm."

"What garbage!"

"Okay," he said solemnly. She was fascinated by his ever-changing performance. "The truth. I must give the truth. Then I will bite down on my cyanide capsule. They plant them cleverly in the lower rear molar, you know. On the left. Did you know that? One of our men accidentally killed himself one time eating a hamburger."

"I didn't know that."

"Oh yes. It's always there, ready for moments like these. The truth." He took a deep breath. "I *adore* you, Natasha. The sun rises and sets with you. I cannot breathe when distances separate us. Poor little Leon Leontovich cries for his mama. The family falls apart without you. Come *home,* Natasha. We *need* you."

"You must stay up nights thinking up this stuff."

"Only once or twice a week. So listen, how d'you like the car?"

"It's beautiful," she said, swiveling to look at the interior.

"Isn't it? This machine's going to be a classic. I take care of it like a baby."

"Touching."

"Seriously. It's going to be worth something. Where do you live?"

She told him.

"Okay. I know where that is," he said, breathing in the faint scent of her cologne, deciding he'd buy her some good perfume. All kinds of things he'd buy for her. But first some perfume. Something to go with her small features, her heavy-looking hair.

"Parents Scandinavian?" he asked.

"My mother's Norwegian. Why?"

"Your hair."

"Oh! Everybody asks me that. It's natural. But you should see my mother's hair. It's almost white. Compared to her, mine's dirty-looking."

"What about your father?"

"French."

"Seaton doesn't sound French," he said.

"Originally, the family name was Saint-Antoine. It got changed to Seaton. What about your family?"

"Nothing. English way back. My father took off when I was a kid. I lived with my mother until I was old enough to get out on my own."

"How old was that?"

"Eighteen."

"Really?" She looked at him with interest. "That's pretty young to be out on your own."

"It kind of depends on which way you look at it. It felt plenty old enough at the time."

"What did you do?"

"Worked, had a scholarship, made my way. No big deal."

"But it is," she said. "It must have been rough, having to work and going to school at the same time."

"Aw, but you're a kindly wee lass, Eileen," he said in a lyrical Irish brogue. "First time I set me eyes upon ye, I said to meself, sure, Paul, that's a kindly wee lass."

"I'm not so wee. And you're a cast of thousands, aren't you?" She smiled again, intrigued by his sudden changes.

"Which house?" he asked in his own, neutral voice.

"Fourth up from the corner on this side."

He pulled over and took the car out of gear.

"Lived here long?" he asked, looking at the tidy brick house.

"Nine years."

"What's your father do?"

"He's on the editorial staff of *The Press.*"

"And your mother?"

"She works there too. It's where they met. She's secretary to the managing editor. She's been there twenty-three years. Papa's been with them twenty-one. I used to work with them during vacations. In the office. I liked it. They're all crazy." She paused, her eyes glinting. "Like you."

He turned her around and looked into her eyes for several seconds before placing his mouth over hers. He was so self-assured it was overpowering. And being held against his chest, having his mouth pressing lightly against hers was too nice to fight against. She touched his cheek. His mouth came away from hers and again he looked into her eyes.

"When?" he asked.

"Tomorrow," she whispered.

He kissed her again, easing her mouth open. Her heart was pounding as her arms slipped around him. Involuntarily. Her arms simply reached out and wound around him as his tongue slid into her mouth and seemed to go darting right down through the center of her body. It was unlike any other kiss she'd ever received. And she might have stayed there indefinitely in the smoky warmth of the car with his tongue moving in her mouth if he hadn't eased himself away and kissed her on the side of the neck, saying, "Tomorrow. I'll pick you up at seven."

Hoarsely, she said, "Yes," and groped for the door handle, then walked, trembling, to the front door and inside. Dazedly, she unbuttoned her coat, listening as he drove away. Thinking. This is it. It was all going to happen. The future was extending an open invitation. She could scarcely bear the idea of having to wait out the next fifteen or so hours. Because, just like that, without even trying, she was in love.

✠   ✠   ✠   ✠   ✠

Two

WHEN HE APPEARED AT THE FRONT DOOR THE NEXT evening, everything inside her seemed to spring to life in recognition. She'd spent almost the entire day thinking about him but until she saw him at the door, she'd been unable to remember what he looked like. Now, his smile, his look of mischief—how could she have forgotten that?—produced a responding smile on her mouth, a ballooning sensation in her lungs.

He shook hands with her father, saying, "Glad to meet you," before extending his hand to her mother.

Margot watched her parents, trying to read their reactions to him. They seemed disarmed by Paul. He was charming, she thought. Surely they felt it too.

At their invitation, Paul stepped into the living room to admire her mother's needlework, the furniture. It was all beautiful, he thought, gratified, pleased with his judgement. These were people of good taste, quiet intelligence. And Margot looked flushed, even prettier tonight in a simply cut black dress.

As they were on their way to the car, he said, "You look terrific!"

"So do you," she said truthfully.

"I thought about you all day," he said, once inside the car. "Didn't do one worthwhile thing, thinking about you." He reached into his topcoat pocket and produced a package. "Thought you'd like this, Louis."

She was unaccustomed to receiving gifts from dates and not sure of the proper response. But proper responses didn't seem to be a necessary part of being with him. She accepted the package and removed the wrapping paper to look at a half-ounce bottle of expensive French perfume.

"Thank you," she said, her heart racing. "You've got a lotta class, junior."

"Like it?"

"I love it," she said, sniffing at the stopper. "You're really okay, you know that, junior?"

"Yeah." He grinned. "You too, Louis. For a guy in drag." He started the car.

She sat with the perfume in its box in her lap, her hand resting on top of it, gazing out through the windshield. Her eyes held an image of her own naked body, the perfume dotted here and there; the scent and her flesh all heated, heavy. She felt intimidated by her imaginings.

"How do you know Suzanne?" she asked casually.

"I know Roy. He was a freshman when I was a senior."

"Oh."

"Ever been to Ginetta's?"

"No. Is that where we're going?"

"Only the best for you, sweetheart." He chuckled and pulled a face at her. "Christ almighty! You look terrific."

"Stop that! You'll give me a swelled head."

He handled everything easily, as if he'd learned to do it all for some other routine she hadn't yet seen; checking their coats, exchanging quips with the headwaiter as if they were old friends, ordering drinks, then lighting a cigarette and leaning forward, beaming at her.

"Okay?" he asked, his eyes scorching hers. She thought of his tongue in her mouth and felt dizzy.

"Great!"

He placed his hand over hers. He loved the shape of her eyes, the slight inward curve of her shoulders, the rise of her breasts beneath the black dress. Lust for her was like a grenade in his belly. Anything at all might cause the pin to be pulled. He could see her spread under him, feel the power inside himself as he made her beg, made her moan. He'd explode inside her. But first, he'd make her crazy to have it.

"You're making me nervous," she whispered, "looking at me that way." She knew what he was thinking, could feel his eyes moving over her. She felt the faintly abrasive pull of her tights against her upper thighs.

"I'm crazy about you, Louis," he said throatily. "You know it. You know where my mind is right now, too."

She lowered her eyes and looked at his hand covering hers, the warmth from it seeping through her skin. Suddenly, perversely, she wanted to cry. She had the feeling she was swimming in water far too deep and was slowly being overcome by exhaustion. Yet, if she stopped for only a moment to rest, to acclimate herself, she'd go under. And, inside this feeling, she had a sudden insight into her parents' role in her life. Mama, Papa, you can only watch me go. You can't keep or protect me. All you can do is stand in the doorway and wave goodbye. This is how it feels to be a woman finally, to know that all the decisions rest within myself. I always wanted to be at this point, to be entirely free to speak and decide for myself. Now I'm here. But the decisions are getting made somehow by themselves. And this man knows something about me. I know what he wants. I want it too. This is love. Isn't it?

She drank, nibbled on a breadstick and tried to stay tuned in to what he was saying. His words seemed to fade in and out as she noticed how unusual his eyes were—light blue with a startling black perimeter. There was something almost animal about his eyes, something primitive.

"You're not listening," he accused teasingly.

"Sorry," she said, blushing. "What were you saying?"

"It's hard enough trying to talk when I'd rather be doing a lot of other things like … Just pay attention, Lou. I'm not gonna get thrown out of another restaurant like we did the last time. And stay off the table, willya? Throwing yourself around. Makes me crazy. You know that? You gotta learn some control."

"You're right. I know you're right. I don't know what comes over me. I get this insane urge and I just gotta get up there and do my Ruby Keeler routine."

He laughed loudly, causing several heads to turn in their direction. "Dance, my Aunt Fanny." He laughed. "You wasn't dancing, sweetheart."

"No? What was I doing then?"

"Jeesus! You mean to tell me you was that drunk?"

"I must've been. I don't seem to remember."

"Okay," he said, dropping his voice. "I'll tell ya. Just so's you don't take it into your head to do nothing like that no more. Okay?"

"Okay."

"See, what you did, you flung your drawers in the Jell-o, Louis. Now, see I toldya at least twenty times, you gonna fling your drawers, fling 'em, *away from the food*." He watched her toss back her head and laugh. "Christ almighty," he said impulsively. "I love you."

She stopped mid-laugh, her eyes connecting with his.

"You mean it," she said, amazed. "How can you mean it? You don't know me. We don't know each other."

"Doesn't matter. What about you?"

"I love you too," she said, thinking, This is a wild, crazy game!

"Let's run away back home, Lulubelle. The ole plantation's jus' fallin' to rack and ruin. Let's us ran away home and raise up a messa kids. Lord, Lord but I miss them grits an' black-eyed peas."

"Don't I know it, though! Ah've had a hankerin' for chit-tlin's for nigh on a montha Sundays."

His hand tightened around hers. "I want to kiss your navel," he whispered.

She exhaled in a rush, her face on fire. Fortunately the food arrived at that moment and he released her hand but continued to hold her eyes with his for several seconds.

The food was wonderful and she wanted to eat but couldn't. She could only watch him, the way he ate, chewed, swallowed. The movement of his hands—smaller than her own, she saw—with carefully trimmed and cleaned fingernails. He broke a bit of bread, buttered it, then lifted it to his mouth. His mouth opened, revealing his pink tongue flatly waiting to receive the bread. His lips closed forming a slight, knowing smile as he acknowledged her eyes on him.

Eating had become a sexual experience and she felt too visible, nervous; wanting nothing to destroy his desire or her own. If she pushed food into her mouth or ate noisily, if she demonstrated a lack of skill and style, he might go, away or change his mind. It was important to keep on being worthy of his desire. His wanting her made her significant in a new way. This man wants me, she thought. This man. He has possessions, a life he has made for himself. Now he wants to possess me too. I had no idea I could yearn to be involved the way I do now.

"You're not eating," he observed.

"It's very good," she said, flustered. "Really very good." She ate several quick mouthfuls as if to demonstrate just how good.

"They do fabulous cheesecake. Like cheesecake?"

"I hate cheesecake," she admitted, smiling, flushing. Falling apart with lust.

"Whatever you want, sweetheart," he said, tough-guy

again. "The sky's the limit."

She ordered *mousse au chocolat*. He had the cheesecake. In silence, they attended to their desserts.

"Now I know how you keep the classy body lines," he said. "Unless it's me taking away your appetite."

"A little," she said honestly. "You're kind of like a tennis match. I'm afraid if I take my eyes away for a minute I might miss the match point."

"Nice. I've never thought of myself quite that way. I'll have to move it around a little, see how it feels. Cigarette?"

"I don't smoke."

"Make a note of that!" he said off to one side, causing her to laugh. "Coffee?"

"Yes, please." She wondered why some of the things he did made her feel embarrassed for him and wondered, too, how she could so easily skirt that feeling and keep on thinking about his wanting to kiss her navel, the way he referred to her body.

"Some after-dinner hootch?" he offered.

"Maybe later."

"Right."

He ordered two coffees and a Drambuie for himself, then pushed his chair back from the table. It was the sort of move she'd seen her father make: a large man's gesture, making room for long legs.

"Dancing?" he asked. "Or something else?"

"I don't really feel like dancing tonight."

"Okay. We'll do something else. Tell me what you do feel like doing."

"I don't know," she lied.

"How about going back to my place?"

Here it comes! she thought, jolted. She hadn't thought he'd get to it so directly. She'd expected him to work up to it gradually.

"All right," she agreed.

She watched him pay the tab, removing several bills from a slim leather billfold. He laid them down over the check before returning the billfold to his inside breast pocket. She liked the cut of his three-piece suit, the Edwardian-looking flare of the jacket, the close-fitting lines of the waistcoat. He looked all of a piece, very carefully put together. Noting his every move, she felt she was disintegrating breaking into dozens of small pieces.

As they drove toward the lakefront and his apartment, she found she was clenching her teeth, battling down sudden fear. She didn't want this encounter to be as disappointing as her two previous ones. The first time was awful and she was sorry afterwards she'd gone through with it. The second time had been to see if she'd been wrong about the first time. It was somewhat better. But only somewhat. She hadn't, until tonight, had any special interest in going out for a third try in order to prove herself wrong in the first two instances. If she went on that way, she might get through dozens of men just trying to see if she'd been wrong about the time before.

✠   ✠   ✠

The view was spectacular, panoramic. From his fourteenth floor apartment, she could look out and see the sweep of the lakeshore as it curved for miles. Lights and distances. The display was mesmerizing her, and the music spread from the corners of the living room to surround her. He placed a balloon glass of brandy in her hand and stood quietly beside her looking down, looking, out, sipping at his drink.

"It's beautiful," she said, turning to take in the details of this place where he lived. It was unexpectedly inviting and comfortable. A long, sleek sofa with pure, clean lines; armchairs upholstered in nubby, rough-woven wool. The colors all muted, subdued. Beiges, creams, a touch of brown, of orange. Two huge plants filled the window behind the sofa. Being a corner apartment, it offered views in two directions. This was the sort of place she'd have liked for herself had she had the money, the independence, the wherewithal to provide it. "How long have you lived here?" she asked, turning back to the window.

"Three years."

If he pulls funny routines now, she thought, I'll die.

They sat together on the sofa. He gave her plenty of room, for which she was grateful. She didn't feel ready. For anything. He could see the brandy taking effect; her cheeks ripe with color, her movements becoming lazier, her smiles more frequent, her speech slower.

"I'm not used to drinking this much," she said with a shy, schoolgirlish smile. "You're going to corrupt me."

"Christ almighty! I hope so. A refill?"

"Sure. Why not?" She held out her glass, dopily watching him get up and carry the two glasses out to the kitchen, hearing the chink of glasses being set down and the splash of liquid being poured into them. She let her head fall back, drinking in the atmosphere, the building tension inside. She was alone here with this man of many voices and comedic routines.

"You're getting tanked," he said, handing her her replenished glass.

"Yup." She laughed, attempting to focus on his face. She sipped at the brandy, feeling it hitting her brain. It wasn't going to her stomach but straight to her brain, anesthetizing it.

He let his arm drop down on her shoulders, his hand playing over her upper arm. Waiting time was over. He had to put his hands on her, touch her. He removed the glass from her hand and set it down on the coffee table, then cupped her chin, holding her face steady as his mouth dropped into place over hers and his tongue swam into her mouth.

She knew she'd dissolve from the heat of her body and the fire his tongue was stoking inside her mouth, over her lips. She couldn't breathe and broke away, saying, "I really can't stay too long."

"It's early," he said, bringing her back, his hand moving off her arm and over the back of her neck, up under her hair. With relief, she sensed he wasn't going to be funny, make any jokes. His hand on her neck burned yet sent shimmering cold spasms the length of her spine.

She shivered when his hand moved down her back. She tightened, tightened, then unbent all at once as his hand moved around over her hip, down across her thigh.

"Let's go into the bedroom," he suggested.

She was without words. He pulled her up and she went with him to the bedroom, to stop just inside the door, making a small, startled sound as he came up behind her and placed his hands over her breasts. He turned her, locking his arms around her, holding her trapped against him as he kissed her throat, her ear, her chin and, at last, her mouth. She had a trembling desire to escape, run before this turned into another disillusioning experience. But he kept on kissing her until she gradually lost her stiffness and relaxed inside his arms, returning the kisses.

"Trust me," he crooned. "You've got to trust me."

"Why?" she asked, dry-throated.

"It's serious."

She wanted to ask him to explain but he bent her backward until she was enveloped by softness, the bed feeling natural, familiar—hadn't she been sleeping in one all her life?—and her reluctance eased. His hand moved slowly under her dress, making its way between her legs. She kept her thighs pressed close together and he stopped kissing her to say, "Don't! You want this." She nodded as his fingers explored along the neckline of her dress.

She caught hold of his hand. "I ..." What did she want to say? "I haven't done a lot of this," she said. "All right?"

He closed his eyes for a moment, thinking, then opened them. "I love you," he said.

She believed him. Absolutely. She did. And released his hand, embracing him. He shifted, pulling her over toward him and as he kissed her, he unzipped her dress, ignoring the protesting sounds she made into his mouth as he pulled it down over her arms, around her waist. Between kisses, he managed to get her slip down around her waist as well. She wasn't helping and he liked that. Anything too easy wasn't worth going after. He investigated the interior of her ear with his tongue, then went back to her mouth. And, finally, her brassiere was unfastened and dangling from her shoulders as his hand moved over her breasts. His fingers teased at her nipples, sending blinding shocks of pleasure through her head, her belly, into her groin. She watched him bend his head to her breast, felt his mouth opening, then closing around the nipple and she sucked in air with a surprised little whimper, feeling wetness gathering at the tops of her thighs.

He went on and on with his mouth at one breast, then the other, while his hands slowly stroked higher and higher inside her thighs. Then he broke away, climbed off the bed and began to undress, peeling away his clothes to reveal a smooth, hairless chest. She shut her eyes as if the sight of his body might render her sightless or mute. When she opened them again, he was naked. And he took hold of her hand and, his eyes glazed, made her put her hand on him. She couldn't look away. Here was proof of something. Proof of what she could do to him? Of what he could do to her? She had no idea. She lay still, stunned, as he stripped away her clothes.

"I knew you'd be great," he said. "Beautiful tits." He smiled, settling on top of her with a satisfied sigh and a look of great contentment on his face. His body, his skin felt so good. She knew he wanted her to open her legs but she couldn't. Not yet.

He began kissing her again, partially sliding off her in order to reach her breasts and belly, to let his hands glide from her breasts down to her thighs, stroking the soft length of her legs, insinuating his hand between them to move higher and higher until her legs parted slightly and his fingers were on her.

He looked at her face, seeing there the expression he'd known he could create. Her eyes wide, glassy. Her mouth open. Every movement of his hands on her body brought sounds from her throat. And once he'd succeeded in getting her to open her legs, she completely lost her resistance. She returned his kisses avidly, twitching as his fingers slid over her, then inside her, probing.

"What do you like?" he asked her. "Tell me. I want to make you feel good."

"I don't know," she whispered, mortified by the question.

She waited to see what he'd do. He lay back down beside her, fastened his mouth to hers and began stroking her rhythmically, his fingers sliding back and forth, generating a desperate, heated excitement inside her that caused her to open herself to it further, lifting. He made her want to scream, to sink her teeth into something. She longed to get away yet still to sink deeper and deeper. She gasped for air, breathing harder, faster as the intensity built and his fingers pressed insistently. His mouth left hers and went to her breast. She clutched his head as her eyes closed and her body squirmed under his hand, moving to make the feeling bigger, better. He had her left leg trapped between his. His mouth sucked at her. His fingers pushed, pressed, stroked. Her fingers wound themselves into his hair, forcing his head to her breast as her breathing turned to gasping cries coming closer and closer together until she went rigid and his fingers kept moving. She pushed him off her breast, dragging his head up to fix her mouth to his as her body flew apart going this way, that way, jolted, shuddering. She kissed him frenziedly as his fingers kept her flying. Until it was done and she closed her legs around his hand and sank under him like a stone, chanting, "I love you Paul I love you. Paul, I love you. *My God!*"

He drew his hand out from between her legs and closed it over her breast, squeezing.

"You make me feel …" She shook her head unable to find an appropriate word. Love. This was it. No doubt. And all at once she was making commitments like crocheted loops in her brain, images of their future together dotting her mind with all the glinting magnetism of spangles in a spotlight.

"You and me, Louis," he said softly, "all the way. Ready for round two?"

Please, she prayed, don't go funny on me! For God's sake don't do one of your routines now.

In order to prevent it from happening, she put both her hands between his thighs, boldly caressing him. And at once he was serious again. He reversed himself and knelt over her, burying his face between her thighs. Taken by surprise—this had never happened before—she lay still for a moment looking at his body swaying above her. Yes! she thought and brought him down to her mouth. To discover she didn't mind doing this. What he was doing was wildly stimulating, so much so, she stopped what she'd been doing and, before she'd even realized she was ready, was coming again. It wasn't as explosive as the first time and didn't last as long. She wished it could have lasted longer.

When he began positioning himself between her thighs, starting to insinuate himself inside her, all her pleasure vanished. She was returned abruptly to an awareness of herself, of what was happening, and was dismayed that there was—like the other times—so little pleasure for her in this.

"I'm not ready," she whispered.

He blinked, losing for a moment his rapt look of concentration, then smiled at her, pausing partially inside her to commence stroking her breasts with both hands. "Enjoy it, Margot," he urged. "Let go and enjoy it."

I don't know how, she thought sadly as he began to move back and forth against her. It actually hurt. His hands went beneath her, raising her. His face was radiant as he looked down to see himself completely joined to her.

"Go with it," he said, his eyes sleepy-lidded, his mouth hungry. "Take it."

She couldn't. She tried to, but didn't know where she was supposed to go. But he'd made her feel so good. So she held him, caressed his arms and made her body as soft as she could as he moved inside her. Yet she couldn't sustain it. Despite the way he'd made her feel before, she wanted this to end and couldn't believe how long it went on. Until her body felt beaten, defeated as he kept on thrusting inside her. Her thighs ached, her insides were being battered. Still he continued. Looking ecstatic. On and on. Until at last his movements accelerated and his hold on her hardened cruelly and he cried out, making her feel guilty for disliking it because he so obviously was deriving the most profound pleasure from her body. He went on, stabbing short and hard inside her, quivering, then subsiding finally in her arms, crying out, "Christ almighty! I love you."

"I love you too," she whispered, cradling his slender body in her arms. "I love you."

It was an odd feeling. She wanted to cry.

Three

I WAS A BALL," HE WAS SAYING, HIS MOUTH DOWN-
turned. "She bounced me off the walls, the furniture. Then
she'd cry and kiss me and say, 'Darling, darling, mummy
didn't mean it. You know I love you. Say you fell, if anyone
asks; you had an accident. You won't forget, will you, darling?' She'd hold me and put ice on the bruises and go on
telling me, 'I didn't mean it. You know I didn't. I love you.
You're my little boy.' And then everything would be special
treats and ice cream, staying up late. Until the next time.
Then she'd punch and kick and bounce me some more. It
all turned slowly until I hated her more than I loved her
and finally just hated her. And by then, I was too big. She
couldn't toss me around anymore. So, the two of us lived in
that house hating each other. I was the one to blame for
everything that'd ever gone wrong in her life. It was my
fault my father left her, my fault when she'd run out of
booze, my fault when the latest guy would take off."

"That's so horrible!" Margot said, appalled.

"Listen, you should try telling a roomful of doctors and
nurses you broke your own ribs by throwing yourself down
the stairs."

"You had to go to the hospital?"

"A couple of times. Once she threw a pot of soup. Lucky
thing for me it hadn't been on the stove long so it was only

very hot, not boiling. Toward the end, they started looking sideways at her when she'd bring me in yet again, telling them, 'He's accident-prone. I just don't know what I'm going to *do* with this boy.'"

"My God! You had to *hate* her!"

"Well," he said in a quieter tone of voice. "I just wanted you to know, so you wouldn't be looking forward to being taken home to meet my mother and all that."

"Were you poor?" she asked, searching for a rationalization.

"Hell! She's got money coming out of her ears. *Poor*. No," he said, more softly still, "We were all kinds of things but not poor."

He kissed her shoulder and looked slowly over her body, touching the taut flesh of her breasts, the swelling softness of her upper thighs. "I love the way your thighs are round right here at the top." He continued stroking her thighs for a moment, then smiled brilliantly. "Let's get married! Right now! Tonight!"

"Are you crazy?" she exclaimed, although the idea fired her with giddy excitement.

"Yeah! Let's do it!"

"You can't be serious! We've seen each other twice."

"Seeing you sixty times wouldn't change the way I feel. I mean it."

"What time is it?" she asked, picturing her mother in bed reading, waiting to hear her come in.

He frowned. "I don't want to have to worry about time with you. I want you to be here every night, all the time. I need you here. We'd be so happy together. Can't you see that?"

"What time is it?" she asked again.

"Almost eleven."

"I thought it was a lot later," she said, relaxing again.

He laughed. "We're getting married!" he declared.

"Tonight. Right after we do this one more time."

He grabbed her greedily into his arms, sighing with the pleasure of holding her. The idea of their eloping filled him intoxicatingly, thrillingly. To do something because it was there to be done. He was positive he could convince her, determined to convince her. Had to. He felt he could get her to do almost anything. He didn't know why. He simply felt it. And he wanted to be married to her, to have her with him always, more than he'd ever wanted anything else. And later on, he'd casually mention her high heels, talk to her about flats. In flats, they'd look the same height. Then, everything would be really one hundred percent perfect.

"This," he said, smiling, his mouth brushing back and forth against hers, "is a little foolproof sample of more of the fantastic technique worked out for me by dozens of hardworking field technicians who positively guarantee its success."

"Don't be funny now," she said softly.

"O-kay!" he said, his mouth swooping down on hers.

He did stimulate her so easily, so completely she thought she might, eventually, get him to cut out his comedy routines altogether when they were making love. Without realizing it, at least until she snatched a moment to think about it, her consent had already been given. Because she was future-thinking about the two of them as a "we."

All too easily, with his kisses and compelling caresses, he elevated her to a state where she was all eager willingness, anxious to try for a second time. To see if it might be better.

He was placing himself between her thighs, preparing once more to put his mouth on her. And she wanted this. This was the most exquisitely piercing pleasure she'd ever known, rendering her mindless, accepting, and as she began tightening, climbing, he righted himself and easily penetrated her. Smiling as she feverishly wrapped her legs around him.

But no matter how long he continued on, she couldn't get herself back to the point of frenzied receptivity she'd been at when he'd entered her. It'll get better as time goes by, she told herself, trying to shift herself to heighten the sensations. As we become more accustomed to each other, this will grow, become for me what it is for him.

Watching his face as he rode above her, she knew she wanted to compensate for his early unhappiness; to make his life so happy from this point on that all that childhood misery would be forgotten, relegated to the past where it belonged. I can make you happy, she thought. Look how happy you are already!

✠   ✠   ✠

They showered together, laughing and tickling each other, got dressed and drove forty miles over the line to be married in one minute and thirty-eight seconds by a justice of the peace with his wife and son in attendance as witnesses.

She telephoned home to say, "I just got married," in a tiny, astounded voice that didn't sound remotely like her own. "I'm going to be home in a week."

Her mother said, "Is this a joke, Margot? You can't be serious!"

"No, no. We did. Paul and I just got married. We're on our way back to the city now."

Her mother let out her breath very slowly, then said, "What is there for me to say? I am too shocked even to think."

Margot knew her mother was terribly upset. It made her feel guilty. Guilty and sorry. Hearing her mother's voice was returning to reality, and reality was the fact that she'd just gone ahead and married someone about whom she knew practically nothing.

She talked a minute longer to her mother, promising to telephone the next day, then hung up and turned to look at Paul who was watching her with an expression containing elation, suspicion and—could she be mistaken?—anger. No, no. He couldn't be angry. He looked happy. He kissed her, grabbed her hand and they ran back to the car where he swung her around, laughing exultantly.

"Christ almighty, Louis!" He laughed and laughed, swinging her around. "We *did* it!"

For just an instant right then, looking at his jubilant features, hearing his laughter, she felt entirely separated from him and wondered what sort of contagious lunacy she'd allowed herself to get caught up in. But it was only an instant. And his happiness was genuine. Her feelings swelled as she was overcome by a mix of protective feelings, motherly feelings, sexual feelings. She was sore, swollen. And just looking at him, she contracted inside—a secret, thrilling internal clenching.

"I love you," she said, fitting herself into his arms. "What do we do now?"

"I'be god a terribuh code im by head. Flu, I think. I'be godda hab to sped a week in bed. At least."

"You've got one for every situation." She laughed.

"Come on," he said, urging her into the car. "I want to get back to the city. I'm hungry, thirsty and hor-nee."

The next morning while she listened, her hand over her mouth to hold back rising giggles, he telephoned his office to do his flu routine. He sounded authentically ill, very convincing. With sniffles, half-stifled sneezes, choked coughs. The complete gamut of symptoms, all perfectly rendered. He hung up and turned to her with that mischievous grin she was learning to know, and chuckled.

"That's that!" He congratulated himself, dropping back down on the bed. "I'm starved," he said, staring at the ceiling. "Hungry?"

"No. But I'll make you breakfast if you like."

"You can cook too?"

"Some. I can certainly handle breakfast."

She got up, pulled on her slip and went out to the kitchen. She loved the feeling of being in this place, belonging here. She felt married and couldn't believe how easily, how effortlessly she'd climbed inside a married feeling, as if it was something that had been waiting for her. Now she was here and she stepped inside the feeling without reluctance, making her way around the kitchen proprietarily.

"We'll have to do some shopping," he said, leaning against the refrigerator, drinking a glass of orange juice as he watched her. "You can't spend a week without a change of clothes. I'll tell you what, Louis, sweetheart. Just to showya where my heart's at, I'll buy you some duds for a wedding present."

"Can you afford it?" she asked, watching the butter melt in the frying pan.

"You let *me* worry about that."

"All right." It seemed logical to assume he could afford to make the gesture or he wouldn't have offered.

She sat opposite him at the table with a cup of coffee and watched him devour four eggs, eight strips of bacon, six pieces of toast, a good half-cup of raspberry jam, two more glasses of orange juice and three cups of coffee. She hadn't believed when he'd told her to prepare that much food that he'd actually consume it all. She'd never seen anyone— especially a man who weighed only about a hundred and fifty pounds, if that—eat so much food at one sitting.

"Do you always eat this much?" she asked.

"Probably have to increase my intake now," he said, lighting a cigarette. "What with all the regular exercise I'll be getting from now on." His smile was curved with sexual meaning.

She blushed but met his eyes. No point in hedging now. After all, sex was a big part of marriage. And she was look-ing forward to it as much as he evidently was.

"Gorgeous," he said, his eyes suddenly heavy-lidded. "You're gorgeous, kid."

"You're not bad yourself, junior."

And off they went back to the bedroom.

Later, lying side by side, sated, she wondered about all that had happened to her in just three days. It seemed, for one thing, far longer than only three days. She'd spent a night in bed—an entire night—with a man for the first time. She'd found it difficult to sleep and stayed awake long after Paul had fallen asleep, looking at him, taking advantage of his sleep to look at his genitals. She'd wanted to laugh, looking at them. But she didn't considering the fact that he might find her body equally amusing.

He took sex so seriously. Everything, she understood, was serious to him. He merely used his routines to mask his seriousness. He wasn't so much a funny man as one with a well-developed sense of humor, a knack of knowing what to say to be amusing. But beneath the funny lines, he seemed to be holding himself away, closely watching every-thing going on around him. Perhaps he'd stop using the routines now that they were married. He'd feel more secure and stop. She didn't dislike them. It was just that she had a very faint suspicion that his habit of falling into different characters might possibly be his way of avoiding issues. But she was probably wrong. She found it so hard to think clearly, to decide on what substances formed the specific essence of the man. He was many things.

She loved being in bed with him, loved the idea of sleep-ing beside him even if she wasn't yet used to sharing a bed. It would come in time. We're married, she thought. We're husband and wife. We're starting a future together.

"You plan to finish up at school?" he asked, interrupting her daydreams.

"I haven't thought about it. But yes. You have to be away at work all day. I might as well finish out the semester and get my degree."

"Why bother? It's not as if you're going to have to use it."

"Maybe not. But my parents did spend an awful lot to see me this far. It seems silly not to go the last few months and get what I started out after."

"Okay," he said, sounding a little displeased.

"You want me to quit," she said, turning on her side to look at him.

"It's just that I don't see the point if you're never going to use it."

"But you never know what can happen. I don't want to let my mother and father down. They're going to have a lot to say about my getting married this way as it is."

"What does that mean?"

"It means what it means. Running off and getting married after one date. They're going to think I've lost my mind. I don't want to upset them any more than I have to. At least if I keep on at school, they'll see I'm not making a whole bunch of wild moves all in one go. They'll see I'm able to make decisions without completely changing my whole life."

"Okay, Louis. If that's what the kid wants, the kid'll get it. Nothin's too good for my old lady."

She smiled and kissed his arm, pressing her mouth to his skin, breathing in his scent, becoming pleasantly drowsy.

"How do you feel about children?" she asked, taking hold of his hand.

"Someday."

"I wasn't planning to start one this week." She laughed. "But how do you feel about them?"

"Don't tell me!" he said, covering her mouth with his

hand, laughing down at her. "Christ almighty, you want six!"

She laughed under his hand. "Maybe one or two," she said lifting his hand away. "Do you feel married?" she asked him, sounding out her new name in her head. Margot Rayburn. Mrs. Paul Rayburn. I'm married. *Married*. This man. Me. We're married. We'll live together. I'll live *here*. With him.

"I feel *good*," he said. "Very very good."

"That's all?"

"I feel terrific, sensational, fantastic. Feeling married'll take another couple of days."

She folded her arm under her head and studied the sunlight patterns on the far wall.

"This summer, when I get my two weeks we'll go somewhere and have a real honeymoon," he said, stifling a yawn. "I'm done," he said, pulling the blankets up from the floor, spreading them over the bed.

"Have a nap," she said. "I think I'll take a shower."

"Wake me when you're through. We'll go out and get you something to wear."

She watched him curl up under the blankets, then turned away and went into the bathroom. Pulling back the shower curtain, she noticed the tiles looked stained. Searching around in the cupboard under the sink she found a sponge and some cleanser. She climbed into the tab, started the water going and scrubbed away, humming to herself, until the walls gleamed. Then, satisfied, she set the cleaning things on the floor beside the tub and stepped back under the shower.

Wrapped in a towel, she returned to the bedroom to see he was still asleep. She tiptoed out and went to the living room to look out first one window, then the other. This is where I'm going to live, she thought, happy. The two of us here with this view. She hugged herself as she stood gazing out at the sunlit waters of the lake.

In the bedroom again, she sat on the side of the bed star-ing down at Paul's sleeping face, thinking, I love you. We're going to be so happy. I can make it up to you for all the good times you didn't have growing up. I know I can make you happy. We'll have such fun together. It wasn't such a crazy thing to do, getting married this way. Other people have done it before. It would seem ridiculous from the outside looking in, but people outside wouldn't under-stand how we feel about each other. They wouldn't know how seeing you makes me feel so soft inside, or how much I really do want to spend all my free time with you.

Guiltily, she thought of her parents and went back to the living room to telephone her mother at her office.

Keeping her voice low, her mother said, "How could you do such a thing, Margot? This is a very serious move you have made. It isn't something to be done lightly."

"Mama, I'm happy. Paul's wonderful. You'll see when you get a chance to know him better. I love him. He's very clever, very funny. He has a very good job."

"Margot," her mother said carefully, "it is impossible to know if you do or do not love someone after only two or three days. You cannot possibly know him. He cannot know you."

She knew her mother's logic was valid but didn't want to listen to logical arguments.

"Don't spoil this, Mama," she said softly. "We're happy."

"We must talk. When will we see you? This is such mad-ness!" she said impatiently. "How did this happen?" She sounded as if she was referring to some catastrophic event that had entirely rearranged her life.

"I'll come next Sunday."

There was a long pause. She could quite clearly see her mother's mouth drawing down, her face assembling itself into irritated planes.

"Your father is most upset," she said, finally.

"Don't do this to me!" Margot said, stricken. "Please! You're making it sound as if I've committed a murder or something. I'm *happy*. I know this is right for me. Oh, I know how it must look to you, but it isn't that way at all. Really, it isn't. Paul and I are right for each other. I love him. You can understand that."

"Oh yes," her mother said tiredly, "I can certainly understand that. You have made the classic North American assumption—the mistaken one—that sexual attraction is love."

"I know the difference."

"No," her mother stated emphatically, "you do not. I must not talk longer. We are very busy."

Margot replaced the receiver and turned with a start to see Paul standing in the doorway. His face was constricted with anger and when he spoke, his lips seemed bloodless.

"Don't you ever apologize for me or anything having to do with me ever again!" Each word shot from his mouth like a bullet.

"I wasn't ..."

"You're my wife. Your loyalty is with me now. If your parents don't like it, fuck *them*!"

"Paul! Don't ... Why are you so angry? I told her I love you. I don't understand why you're acting this way."

He continued to glare at her for several seconds, then let out his breath slowly, saying, "I'm always a wild animal when I wake up. Forget it happened, eh?" He held his hands out to her and tried to smile.

Confused, she got up and allowed herself to be drawn against his chest.

"A little something to remember—learning things about each other—I wake up," he said lightly, his hand smoothing her hair, "like a bear."

"I won't forget," she said, meaning it. "I promise never to

say one word to you until you've been awake at least an hour."

"Right!" he said, kissing her hard before releasing her. "Let me grab a quick shower and then we'll go out."

He went into the bathroom and she stood feeling the panic ebbing inside. He'd frightened her. She had no experience dealing with anger. Particularly irrational anger. And Paul had definitely, for those few minutes, been irrational.

Shrugging it off, she began to straighten the bed when he ducked his head around the bathroom door to say, "Christ almighty, Louis! I need sunglasses in here now. That's terrific! I was going to get around to it some day. Good girl!"

"Hurry up!" She smiled over at him. "I'm getting awfully sick of this dress. I want some jeans and a shirt."

While he showered, she stood by the bedroom window brushing her hair with his hairbrush, concentrating on pushing away a small voice that kept insisting, You've made a mistake. A big mistake. And there's nothing you can do about it now. She fought down the thought, telling herself all newly married couples have misunderstandings until they learn each other's patterns. It isn't a mistake.

Four

HE WAS VERY GENEROUS, INSISTING ON BUYING HER two of everything she liked. She accepted, her convictions strengthening, minute by minute. This marriage was going to be wonderful. She'd found someone who not only wanted her but wanted to give her things, tangible proof of his feelings. She wished she had more to give him but had to satisfy herself with dreams of her future munificence. In time, she'd be able to reciprocate. For now, it was like a fairy tale or a movie.

She wasn't looking forward to re-introducing Paul to her parents on Sunday. They might show their disapproval, might state their unhappiness and thereby upset Paul. She didn't want anyone upset. Trying to anticipate her parents' responses, she had to believe they'd run true to form and display only their usual open-mindedness. She was right.

They were cordial, congratulatory, and Paul was his usual outgoing self, so the initial tension melted away. By the time he and Margot began carrying her hastily packed bags out to his car, next Sunday's dinner together was being arranged and Paul was assuring them he and Margot would come.

It's going to be all right, Margot told herself, embracing her parents before leaving. They'll get used to him, to the idea that we're married. He'll get used to them and see I owe them loyalty just as I do him. Things would be fine. She was going to have a marriage as good as her parents'. Paul was intelligent, imaginative, humorous. He was on the rise in his career. She was going to be his completing half; he would be hers.

Early every morning, she prepared Paul's breakfast and her own cup of coffee, then gathered together her books and hurried down to the bus stop. She used the forty-five minutes of the ride downtown to study. In the afternoons, riding back, she planned their dinner and rushed from the bus to the nearby supermarket to collect groceries. By the time Paul came in, she'd be changed and dinner would be cooking on the stove.

On the weekends, they ate out, went to the theater, the movies or dancing, spending Sunday afternoons with her parents. As the first months passed, routines were established, and she settled happily into them. They were building their life together, laying down the foundations. She was aglow with optimism, with the success of her small efforts thus far. Their reunion at day's end was something they both anticipated eagerly, meeting at the apartment door with embraces and laughter.

Although she was gradually becoming familiar with Paul's comedic approach to most situations, she nevertheless responded with laughter. He was really very clever. He'd dubbed her Louis and most frequently played his tough-guy role, performing it to perfection even down to the studied movements and stylized gestures of 1940 movies. She called him junior and played B-girl, having fun. Fun. Marriage was such fun. They seemed to spend the major part of their time together laughing, even in bed where laughter now seemed a proper part of their activities.

When school ended she was relieved, finally, not to have to spend ninety minutes a day traveling to and from the heart of the city. She was able to do the grocery shopping at her leisure, to spend relaxed hours in the basement laundry room reading while the towels and sheets and their clothes got themselves clean. She mopped and dusted and scrubbed their three rooms and found any number of little things to do to keep herself occupied.

In July, as Paul had promised, they went off for a two-week vacation to the Virgin Islands. They returned home tanned and trim from all the swimming, tennis, beach-walking and strenuous lovemaking. Her diploma arrived, and she tucked it away promising herself she'd one day have it properly framed to hang on the wall of the house Paul was talking about buying for them.

He never again spoke of his mother and although she was curious to know more about his childhood, no amount of subtle hinting would bring him to discuss it. "I'm doing my damnedest to forget I ever knew her," he'd say. "Just pretend I'm an orphan. I think of myself that way."

What she knew of his childhood formed a melancholy pocket in her mind and, occasionally, when something he said or did seemed to make no sense whatsoever, she delved into that pocket for justification. It was only to be expected, she thought, that having undergone so much trauma in his early life he'd perform irrationally now and then. And, on reconsideration, how was she to know what was or wasn't irrational? Living with someone, being married, wasn't something she'd done before. Existing in such close quarters was bound to produce certain pressures. She felt them herself. So, if he did sometimes say things like, "Your shoes are some kind of superiority symbol," she put it down to the pressure of coexistence and bought shoes he liked, with lower heels. When he said, "You don't make any noise when you come. You're holding back," she thought about it and decided he was probably right and made a conscious effort to cry out. That the effort deprived her of some of her pleasure seemed unimportant. What was important was making the marriage work, making Paul happy. Compromise. It cost her little.

In September he received a promotion and a substantial raise and they celebrated by going out for a lavish dinner and dancing afterward at an exotically mirrored discotheque. She wore a dress Paul had bought her, one woven of metallic threads. And felt wickedly, wildly high as they danced and Paul's eyes moved from her to her various reflected images. They both had a lot to drink and flew home to throw off their clothes with drunken laughter and sudden, rapacious seriousness as they fell together on the bed. The accumulated excitement of the evening combined with Paul's demanding hands, mouth and body succeeded in lifting her to a state of sexual greed she hadn't known before. She came for the first time that night with Paul inside her. Ecstatic, proud, she descended from her orgasm into sleep. Paul remained where he was for quite some time studying her, feeling tremendously potent, powerful. He'd done it. He'd do it again. Rolling the idea around in his mind, examining it like some exquisitely cut gem, he disengaged himself and sank his fingers into her, exploring the slick elasticity of her body. He continued on for several minutes before withdrawing his hand, turning over on his side and pitching headlong into a thick, dreamless sleep.

He gave her fifty and then sixty dollars a week for household expenses. It was far more than she needed and she began depositing part of this money in the savings account her parents had started for her when she was a year old. She had all kinds of plans for the money. Furniture for the house Paul was daily growing more determined to have. Or maybe the education of their future children. She kept it secret, thinking she'd one day surprise him and win his additional praise at how cleverly she managed.

After the novelty of free time began wearing off she found

herself becoming bored spending day after day alone in the apartment. Occasionally, she'd take the bus into town to have lunch with Suzanne or another friend, or go shopping at Hamilton's downtown. She'd browse through the University Bookstore, encountering former classmates who were continuing on toward their graduate degrees. She envied them. She loved the atmosphere at the University, missed the conversations, the heated debates.

Throughout the fall she thought about it and in December approached Paul on the subject of resuming her education.

"I thought I might enroll for the spring semester and start work toward my Master's. There's really not enough here to keep me busy all day."

"Are your parents going to finance this?" he asked.

"I haven't thought that far."

"Well, they won't!" he said with certainty. "They've done their bit. So it means if you want to go back to school, I'm the one who's going to have to foot the bill for your tuition, the books, all of it. What's it for, Margot? What're you going to do with an MA?"

"Improve my brain. Learn."

"You're twenty-three. Are you planning to become a perpetual student?"

"What's my age got to do with it?" she countered.

"The way I see it, you'll get your Master's. Then you'll spend a few months around here getting itchy again and the next thing I know, you'll be wanting me to finance your way through a Ph.D."

"Would that be so terrible? With a Doctorate, I could get a very good teaching position, even do research, contribute some money. You'd get paid back for your investment. It might take some time ..."

"You're hung up on that academic bullshit," he accused. "The whole cloistered status. That's not the world, you

know, Margot. The world is out here. You don't want to
grow up. You want to stay a schoolgirl and get a whole
string of status-symbols to tack at the end of your signature.
What're you trying to prove? Or is it that you don't want
to face the fact that we all have to grow up sooner or later?"

"Prove? I'm not trying to prove anything," she said rea·
sonably. "The truth is you're against my going back. Why
don't you just say that instead of making a lot of accusations you know aren't true?"

"You go back and it means putting off having a house for
at least two more years. We're talking about six or seven
thousand dollars, you know."

"I love this apartment," she said, looking around. "I
wouldn't mind one bit spending two more years here."

She wanted to say she'd use her own money for the
tuition. She had enough in her savings account.

"You're too damned self-centered. You expect too much."

"All right," she said quietly, "I'll make a deal with you.
We stay on in the apartment for two more years. I'll pay my
own tuition. That way, I get what I want and you'll have
another six thousand to put toward your house—*our* house.
That's fair."

"Great! And how do you propose paying?"

"Let me work it out, all right?"

He looked at her questioningly, trying to think where
she'd get the money. She'd hit up her parents, obviously.
Well okay, he thought. Let them get stuck paying for you.

"Okay," he gave in. "Enroll. Go back to school. Just don't
complain to me when the walls start closing in on you
here."

"Paul"—she slid over to him—"I'm perfectly happy here.
Don't you want me to do what gives me satisfaction? I like
learning, studying. It certainly can't hurt me to further my
education. And it can't hurt you if I do. Besides, it's lonely
here all day by myself. At least I'll have people to talk to ..."

"Don't overstate your case. You've made your points, But I don't suppose it's occurred to you that I might be getting kind of fed up with this apartment. You've been here only a year. It's more than four years for me. That's a long time to spend in three small rooms."

"But people have lived whole lives in places smaller than this. Not as nice, either. How can you feel that way? This is a beautiful apartment. I thought you thought so too." She could feel the argument sliding into areas unrelated to the issues and couldn't seem to find any way to prevent it happening.

"I want my own place," he said stubbornly. "I'm sick of paying rent. And I don't give a shit how many people've spent their lives in apartments smaller than this. Your logic leaves a lot to be desired, you know."

You're totally illogical, she thought, but stopped herself from saying it.

"Look," she said gently, "I'm very happy here. I'm happy with you. Let's just stay as we are. It's not going to be any different from the way it was before. I'll still be here every night. Your dinner will be waiting for you. Nothing's going to change. Except that I'll be doing something that's good for me."

"How about," he proposed, "doing something that's good for me?"

He stretched his legs out in front of him and she read his face, unable to fully believe he was bargaining with her in this fashion. But his attitude, the expression on his face were unmistakable. He wanted her to demonstrate her recognition of his generosity. She had the distinct and upsetting feeling that if she didn't do what he was silently asking her to do, they'd have an unpleasant argument.

He stretched again, lifting his hips slightly and she watched him, staggered that he could want her to make payment in this fashion. But he did. His eyes were locked to hers, forcing his meaning. Tentatively, she put her hand in his lap and his eyelids drooped slightly, his mouth turning upward fractionally at the corners, his lips parting. She watched his tongue lick his lower lip, then slip back into his mouth and told herself, It's fair. He's delaying a dream of his so that I can fulfill one of mine. So it is fair. But why do I feel this has turned into a nightmare?

She unzipped his trousers and he said, "Wait a second," and opened her shirt, unfastened her brassiere. "Take them off," he whispered. She did, then knelt in front of him feeling more naked than she'd known it was possible to feel. He closed his eyes, his hands under her breasts, guiding her forward. Taking a deep breath, she lowered her head to his lap.

She gagged, coughing, and got up to walk slowly—don't rush away from him! her interior voice warned—to the bathroom, tears coursing down her cheeks as she closed and locked the door. She sobbed painfully as she rinsed her mouth, then brushed her teeth. She kept the water running for several minutes after she'd finished, struggling to get herself back under control. Telling herself, There's nothing to cry about.

She reached for a tissue and blotted her eyes, staring at her reflection in the mirror. I'm going back to school. I have everything I want and need. This was nothing I haven't done lots of times before.

No. It wasn't that they hadn't engaged in other, similar performances. It had to do with the way he'd led her by the breasts, his hands fastened to her; his hands stating the rhythm, guiding her back and forth. By the breasts, as if she was some sort of animal or machine. She'd felt utterly removed, unpleasantly separated from any emotional closeness to him.

Forget it! she told her reflection. If he knew you felt this way, he'd be very upset. He wouldn't intentionally try to make you feel bad. Paul loves me. I love him. And he did-n't go for his graduate degree. He couldn't afford it. So he probably feels I'm getting something he hadn't the oppor-tunity to provide for himself. It isn't fair of me to flaunt the fact that I'm in a position to get additional education. I have to remember all he's been through to get to where he is now. He'd never purposely hurt me. Never. I'm being childish.

✠   ✠   ✠

On the last day of the spring semester, she arranged to meet her mother for lunch. As Margot neared the restaurant, she caught sight of her mother approaching and stopped to watch her. She saw her mother suddenly in an entirely new way, as if Ingrid were a stranger. A tall, straight-backed blonde woman with finely formed features and round, intelligent brown eyes. Long-legged, lean-hipped, broad-shouldered, small-breasted. An arresting handsome woman who moved with purpose. My mother. Margot ran forward to throw her arms around her mother and press her cheek to hers.

"I'm so happy to see you," Margot said, her throat feeling choked. "You look wonderful, Mama."

"You look a little tired," her mother smiled and put her arm around Margot as they went into the restaurant. "How are your studies?" she asked as they settled themselves at their table.

"Good. I'll make good grades."

"And Paul?"

"He's fine. How's Papa?"

"He complains of being tired. He has chest pains."

"Has he been to see the doctor?"

"He will go Tuesday. You know how stubborn he is. He has no respect for medical people."

"But that's ridiculous! If he's sick, he has to get himself taken care of."

"It would be a very good world if all the sick people had themselves taken care of."

There was more than just casual observation to the remark and something warned Margot not to pursue the matter. She picked up her wineglass and sipped thoughtfully.

"You have changed," Ingrid said, her eyes traveling over her daughter's face. "Very much."

"Have I?"

"You avoid issues now. It is something you would never do before."

"What issues? I don't avoid anything."

She found it difficult meeting her mother's eyes. The light in them was so intense, so insistent it was like being x-rayed.

"Who is paying for your tuition?" her mother asked.

"I am," Margot admitted.

"You are. With your savings?"

"That's right."

Ingrid sighed and shook her head. "Why didn't you ask us? The money has always been there for your education."

"I didn't think you should. It doesn't seem fair to keep on asking you to finance me when I'm no longer your responsibility."

"You will always be my responsibility, your father's. What a stupid thing to say! Do you think responsibility for a child ends simply because the child lives away from home?"

"I'm not a child!"

"You are *my* child! You will *always* be my child! That is *my* responsibility. A woman doesn't have a baby, make sure it grows up healthy and then dismiss it. It is for a lifetime, Margot. Surely you cannot be so limited in your insights. I wish you had asked us."

"What difference does it make? I've got the money. I don't see the difference."

"It isn't a matter of the money. It is a matter of our relationship, of our family. In this last year, I can feel you being drawn away from us in so many ways. Of course you have a new life, your marriage. But this is another matter. I can see you don't wish to talk about this."

"You're trying to say Paul's taking me away from you. And that's not true."

"No? Margot, every Sunday the two of you come to visit. All the time you are with us, your eyes are watching him as if he was a naughty child and you are frightened he will break something, or say something, or do something. He is your husband. You have chosen him. But he is not an open man, not a genuinely amusing man, not a man who likes people very much. He does not like us. And you know it. I can live with it. I can live with many things. But can *you* live with it? Do you tell yourself stories? This man is making a battle with us over you. And you are trying to ride in the middle. It cannot be done. If it would be easier for you not to come, we would understand. It seems to me you are taking a difficult course in attempting to remain in the middle this way."

"None of that's true," Margot argued. "Don't you want us to come?"

"Don't behave stupidly, Margot." Ingrid shook her head sadly. "I have never known you to behave this way. Tell the truth! Think the truth! Are you happy? Can you say to me, I am happy?"

"I love him," she said softly. "Don't make this an inquisition. Please. I was so happy to see you."

"Perhaps I am wrong," Ingrid said gently. "I wanted to present you with an opportunity to speak your mind. There is no mistake we can make that cannot be remedied. But I will say nothing more. I am upsetting you."

That was true. The meeting left Margot unsettled, distracted. Paul would never try to come between her and her
family. He was different, didn't easily fit in with them. And
her mother and father were aware of it. But that didn't
mean he wanted to destroy her feelings for her parents or
remove her from them. He'd never said anything about
them. Odd! she thought, realizing that. Aside from that
one comment he'd made the morning after they were married, he'd never again made any sort of reference at all to
her mother and father. He made it seem as if he thought of
her as an orphan the way he thought of himself. He probably couldn't help it. After a childhood like his, all parents
were bound to appear suspect. And he had a right to expect
demonstrations of her love. So why was she so hung up on
that incident? Why couldn't she put it entirely out of her
mind?

She did try. But every so often, when she least expected,
a forbidding darkness seemed to settle over her and she'd
see it all again, experiencing a kind of panic at the memory of the way he'd stretched himself out, the way he'd led
her by the breasts. It had been the one completely loveless
incident of their marriage, the one time she'd entered into
a sexual performance with him without feeling. A bill to be
paid. A debt to be made good in advance. An obligation.
And as a result—evidently a direct one—she was again
unable to reach a climax while he was inside her. He
seemed perfectly content to make her come with his hands
or mouth. And she was becoming convinced that she simply couldn't become completely aroused except manually
or orally. Which was fine. Because Paul would always make
sure she was satisfied before continuing on toward his own
satisfaction. Their lovemaking pattern became established
around his bringing her to a climax, then entering her to
work toward his own. Having established this pattern, neither of them sought to change it. She did think about

experimenting but felt too uncertain about her own responses to suggest it. She concluded that she probably wasn't built quite in the right way to facilitate vaginal orgasms. Although she wasn't sure there could be such a thing. In any case, she kept her doubts to herself and they got through their second year of the marriage relatively peacefully.

Every so often, Paul would make what she regarded as one of his senseless remarks, and she'd try to make sense of it in whatever way she was able in order to keep him happy. The remarks themselves seemed so pointless that she was often more amused than irritated. When he commented on her preferred outfits for attending classes—jeans with a shirt and sweater—saying, "You're working at being a little boy, hiding the woman under your fly," she merely laughed and said, "You know I'm not a little boy," and the remark was so laden with sexual overtones that he stripped her out of the jeans and made love to her standing up in the kitchen as if to prove how well he did know what she was.

✠   ✠   ✠

Having been ordered by his physician to slow down, take things easier, her father, by that following summer, looked more rested, more relaxed than he had in years. Relieved, Margot too relaxed and increasingly enjoyed their Sunday visits.

Paul had fallen into the habit of spending the better part of the morning in the living room with the weekend paper while Margot and her parents sat at the kitchen table drinking coffee, eating fresh-baked Danish pastries and bringing each other up to date on their views of world affairs.

Sundays were the days Margot came to look forward to with increasing dependence. Her parents seemed to be monthly assuming ever more highly unique, tremendously individual attributes in her eyes and the more time she spent with them the more devotedly she loved them. She valued their fairmindedness, their openness to new ideas. Because of their work on the paper, they seemed exceptionally well-informed on all sorts of issues, and Margot sat, with her hands closed around her coffee cup, listening intently to whatever they had to say. Invariably, their conversations were impersonal, general in nature. Margot sensed that the two of them had agreed not to ask her direct questions about her life or her marriage. She was in part grateful and in part sorry. There were times when she wished they'd come right out and ask what they wanted to know. She thought she might to able to answer truthfully. But then she'd remember Paul in the living room and be relieved that they didn't ask. She sensed that Paul was listening, despite the fact that he was two rooms away, and his listening inhibited her. She freely volunteered her opinion on any number of subjects, but when it came down to her personal life, this openness evaporated.

After coffee, her father usually went out to the garden. Margot then would tie an apron around herself and help her mother prepare the Sunday dinner. The late mornings seemed to be full of warmth. Serenity cloaked their words and movements as they readied the meal. From time to time, she'd stop what she was doing to look at her mother; watching her as she talked, hearing her words, gathering their meaning to herself sadly, with a sense of impending loss. She wasn't going to have them forever. There was something too vulnerable about the softening skin of Ingrid's throat, the deepening lines around her eyes and mouth.

God! she'd think, gripped by fear. Don't die on me! Live for me, I need you.

She'd move to the kitchen window to gaze out at her

father's bent back as he weeded and pruned, feeling a liquid column of love pouring through the center of her
being. She'd turn back, sunspots blurring her vision, and
continue whatever she'd been doing.

She couldn't understand the change in her feelings.
Instead of growing less dependent with time, she was
becoming even more dependent upon these two people
whom she admired and respected. Their lives meant more
to her than anyone else's, even Paul's. She shuddered, realizing that if someone was to be lost to her, she could more
easily lose Paul than her mother or father.

Horrified, she tried to reason this through. What's wrong
with me? she asked herself. I love Paul. He's good to me,
generous. We have fun together. She shook her head, trying to bring her considerations down to a more specific
level. Overstating cases. Paul claimed she did this often.
What she was doing now was just another example of her
natural tendency to be overemotional. I'm too old to be
clinging still to my mother and father. We all have to die.
And they're getting older. Her father was fifty-three, her
mother fifty. But when she looked at them critically, they
seemed an impossible mix of old and young. Their attitudes
and opinions were youthful, but the reality showed in their
wrinkling skins and aging bodies. It seemed so unfair that
she should arrive at her full capacity for loving them when
they were inching along to the end of their lives. Paul,
with his gag routines and hard, muscular body was someone it would take her years and years to know. Unfair. Why
did it have to take so long to understand people, to appreciate how much you needed them for your life? She needed Paul for her life, she thought; but not to the same extent
she now felt she needed her parents. She wanted them for
as many years as they had left; wanted to see them, hear
their words, absorb the complete sense of them so that
when they were finally lost to her, they'd continue to live

on within her.

She was inundated by nostalgic memories and the longing to keep her parents forever. Why, she wondered, was she suddenly dreading the thought of losing these two people she'd quite casually accepted for nearly twenty-five years? She didn't know. She knew only that each visit home was vitally important. And Paul knew it too. He offhandedly suggested skipping a Sunday visit, saying, "We could take a run into the country, get some fresh air." She discouraged him. They went to visit her parents. A few weeks later, on a Friday night, he proposed a weekend trip to the seashore and she was about to agree to it when she saw it would mean forgoing her visit home. So she said no.

"Did it ever occur to you that I might prefer spending one of my two free days of the week alone with you instead of with your parents?" he asked.

"But it's *my* only chance to see them. Be reasonable, Paul. They're all I've got, next to you. I'm not going to have them forever. I want to be with them as much as I can while I've still got them."

"And what about me?" he flared. "I'm supposed to just hang around getting old waiting for your mother and father to drop dead?"

Words failed her. She stared at him, unable to believe he could be as jealous as he evidently was.

"I'm telling you right now, Margot. I don't plan to go on indefinitely spending my Sundays over there. You want to go, go alone! I'll be damned if I'll waste one day out of every week sitting around reading the newspaper while the three of you bullshit the day away. You want to go, take the fucking bus! I've got better things to do with my free time."

"Doesn't it matter to you that they're important to me? I love them and I want to be with them. Why can't you accept that and respect my feelings? I don't know why we're arguing."

"I'm your family too, in case you've forgotten. Isn't there room inside there somewhere," he tapped his forefinger hard against the side of her head, "for a little respect for *my* feelings? Or am I just the patsy who supports you? I'm getting pretty goddamned few returns for my money, lady!"

"Returns. For your money. You didn't buy me, you know! Why do you have to reduce everything to money? Money's nothing! The people I love are important. *You're* important. But for some reason I just can't see, you resent my feelings for my mother and father. My mother didn't beat me up, Paul. She loved me and listened to me and tried to help me grow up into a reasonable, loving human being. I'm truly sorry you had such an awful childhood but there's not a hell of a lot I can do to change it, and I don't think your childhood or your experiences with your mother give you a license to try to wipe out the love I share with my parents."

She knew the instant she referred to his mother she'd made a grave error. His face contorted with rage and she just got her last word out when his hand flew up and collided with her cheek. Shocked, she reeled backward, gaping at him. Her mouth open, she lifted her hand slowly to her face. Then she whirled around and raced for the door but he got there first, words spilling from his mouth.

"Margot! I'm sorry, I'm sorry." His eyes distraught, his mouth trembling, he said, "I'm sorry. I didn't mean to do it. Christ, I didn't!"

"Get out of my way!" she said, refusing to look at him, trying to reach past him to the doorknob.

"Margot," he begged, his hand falling on her forearm. She shrugged it off.

"Let me by!" she said, struggling to keep her voice flat, unrevealing.

"*Please!*" he pleaded, his chest heaving. "I'm sorry. I'm *sorry!*"

She looked up to see his eyes were filling with tears. He was going to cry. She couldn't believe any of this was happening.

"You don't have to hit people to make points, Paul. And you don't hit *me*!"

"I'm sorry," he said again, his voice emerging thin as a thread. "I don't know how it happened. I don't know why." Tears spilled over the rims of his eyes and the sight of them defused her anger. Wearily, she stepped away, turning her back on him and walking slowly into the living room. She looked down and saw that she was grinding her hands together. She separated them as if they were two brawling animals, letting them fall to her sides where they hung twitching, fidgeting. Her heart was banging noisily, her eardrums throbbing. What was happening here? She'd pressed a dangerous button, dragged up vile memories, and he'd retaliated, blindly striking back. She'd brought this blow upon herself. He came up behind her, putting his hand on her shoulder.

"Please, can we forget it?" he asked, his voice strained.

Ashamed of herself for provoking him, ashamed of him for being provoked, she turned and hid her face against his shoulder. "I love them, Paul," she cried, holding on to him. "Don't resent them because I love them. They don't resent my love for you."

"I'm sorry, I'm sorry." He kept on repeating it throughout the evening, making her feel guiltier each time he did.

At last, they fled to the bedroom to throw off their clothes and make desperate love, both of them seeking a quick route to forgetfulness. She held him while he thrust into her, wishing this were as sure a path to oblivion for herself as it was for him. While he slept, she smoked one of his cigarettes, drank a large tumbler of neat whiskey and tried to convince herself this sort of thing happened at least once in every marriage. She tried hard. But she couldn't quite make herself believe it.

Five

Paul, FEELING PROFOUNDLY GUILTY AS WELL AS CON-
founded by his behavior, endeavored to make amends. He
stopped scouting out ways to get out of the Sunday visits to
her parents and made an active effort to involve himself in
the discussions at the kitchen table. Yet a reserved part of
him still resented the amount of thought and emotion
Margot directed toward them. He wanted her entirely to
himself, wanted to be the pivotal focus of her life. And he
couldn't be. Because her mother and father were always
there, in the background of her thoughts, of her awareness,
of her life. He couldn't force her to stop caring for them.
This reality frustrated and defeated him.

He tried to tell himself it was childish, unworthy of him
to feel the way he did. After all, Margot was his. He had
legal claim to her; was the rightful owner of her flashing
eyes and restless energy. She was his to touch, to hold, to
penetrate, to please. He could do anything with her he
wished. Knowing he had access to her body—and via her
body, her mind—charged him with lust, power. Secure
inside her body, he felt potent, invincible. But away from
her, at a distance, he sat behind his desk and wondered
what she did all day long at the university, whom she saw,
what was said. Did she discuss him, their marriage, with her
friends, her parents? The idea of her revealing intimate

details of their life enraged him. She had no right to tell other people about the things the two of them said and did in private. He sensed she wouldn't. But he couldn't help thinking she might, upon occasion, seek to confide in Suzanne or Ingrid. She might admit she was upset, might tell people he'd hit her. He went cold and tense at the thought.

He concentrated on trying to allow her freedom, breathing room. Yet when she availed herself of the freedom, he felt inexplicably hurt and perplexed. He wanted her to choose to be with him, not to go seeking out friends, her parents, outside activities. He didn't do it. Why should she?

He played tennis one night a week with three other men from the office. This constituted his entire outside social life away from Margot. The rest of his free time was dedicated to her. But she didn't seem grateful.

They went out to dinner at least once a week, saw plays and films often and made love almost nightly, more frequently on weekends. He knew, couldn't help but know, that his being inside her wasn't nearly so pleasurable for her as it was for him. Yet he had the feeling that if he kept on hard enough, long enough, he'd crack her reservations, smash her with pleasure. She was willing to give herself, often playing the aggressor; easily arousing him, then satisfying herself by riding her way into paroxysmic orgasms while straddling his hips and simultaneously manipulating herself. He'd watch her do it, deriving a decidedly distant pleasure from the tightly heated intensity of her movements. But he felt left out. He preferred being dominant, on top.

There were moments when he found himself abruptly, jarringly cut off from her. Engaged physically, disengaged mentally, he viewed her from faraway, almost hating her for the groaning pleasure she was deriving not from his efforts but her own. He wanted to pluck her hand from between their bodies and tie her two hands together above her head, thereby forcing her to receive her pleasure directly from him.

What's wrong with me? he'd ask himself, telling himself how much they loved each other; fearfully questioning the sadistic thoughts that sidled through his mind.

Doubts and suspicion ate away at him. And restlessness. The feeling that changes—of setting, of circumstance—would alter their performances with each other. He had to get them out of the apartment, into a house. A home of his own had come to symbolize more than just financial security. It would mean, he was convinced, seeing Margot more settled. With a home of her own to tend to, she'd understand, see the areas where she was failing and stop this foolish education business and start acting like a proper wife.

They began house hunting on evenings and Saturdays at his insistence, spending months rejecting one house after another for varying reasons—all Paul's. The places were too small, or in the wrong neighborhood. She'd have settled for several of the ones they saw, finding them perfectly suitable, more than adequately spacious. But Paul was after something special and relentlessly he continued the search, determined to find it; determined to keep looking until he did. She was becoming less enthusiastic as he became more determined, and finally the house became a point of contention. She couldn't see why he so adamantly refused to compromise.

"I'm not going to live in a cracker-box in some treeless, godforsaken suburb with a bunch of blue-collar slobs! We're going to have a house with something to it in a town with something more going for it than a railway spur."

She shrugged. "You're looking for something mythical. We're going to have to settle, Paul. You know it doesn't matter to me. I've told you that over and over again. It'd be fine with me if we moved to a larger apartment. My parents did that. They waited. If you can't find what you want now, why don't we compromise and wait another year or two until we have a bit more money and you can buy what you want?"

"First of all," he said with a fatigued, impatient air as if she was being impossibly stupid, "I don't give a shit what your *parents* did. And secondly, real estate values are skyrocketing. Another year or two and we won't even be able to afford the crapcans that're overpriced now as it is."

"Listen, junior," she said, trying to appeal to his sense of humor, "when the time's right, the perfect hideout'll come along. The guys don't complain. The guns're stashed safe here. And nobody'll ever find the money under the floorboards."

"Louis, Louis," he shook his head. "Christ almighty, I hoped you wouldn't find the money."

"Junior." She smiled, eased. "You know I wouldn't tell nobody. You know that." What's going to happen, she wondered, when this routine doesn't work anymore? When I can't find any more ways to get through to you? "Paul," she said softly, "I don't need a house. I'm happy here the way we are. Can't you forget it for a while? Does it really matter that much having a house?"

"I want it," he said, his face filled with a child's petulance and stubbornness. "You're doing the things you want, Margot. This is something *I* want."

"Okay," she demurred. "We'll keep looking. Obviously, it means a lot to you." I can see that but I can't make sense of it. What is it you're *really* looking for?

✠   ✠   ✠

The search continued. For months they spent their evenings riding around in brokers' cars looking at houses.

Exhausted, Margot would drag herself out of bed in the morning to prepare for the day. There were times when she wished she'd never gone to Suzanne's party, had never seen or spoken to Paul. But almost every time she'd guiltily entertain these thoughts, Paul would do something— arrive home with flowers or a piece of jewelry—to make her feel even more guilty and disloyal. So to compensate, she'd be even more attentive, accompany him on yet another fruitless search of the suburbs.

The idea that she'd made a mistake in marrying Paul haunted her. She refused to accept that possibility, hating the thought of the remarks that might be made—by her parents, by Suzanne who'd lifted her eyebrows at the news of the marriage. No, she'd make it work. She loved Paul. He loved her. There was no mistake.

Two years after the search had begun, Paul looked at and liked a house in an expensive town on the direct train-line about forty miles from the city. A commuter town of great charm with houses bordering the river and a scattering of artists, authors and actors who'd chosen to live there. The house itself was old, enormous, in magnificent condition, on three-quarters of an acre of land.

"It's far too big for the two of us," Margot commented.

"This is it!" he said, running his hand over the old polished paneling of the den. "I'm making an offer."

She bit back further comment, not wanting to have an argument with him in front of the broker. But the minute they arrived back at the apartment, she had to speak out.

"That house is all wrong for us," she said, prepared to discuss the issue calmly. "And besides, it would bankrupt us."

"I'm the one who's going to pay for it, so leave that end of it to me."

"Paul, don't treat me like a brainless adolescent. *I'm* the one who'd have to clean that place and keep it up. We don't *need* five bedrooms and four bathrooms. We don't *need* a living room *and* a sitting room *and* a den. Not to mention a baronial dining room and a butler's pantry. Our furniture would disappear in those rooms. It would cost us a fortune just to furnish that place."

"We're buying it!"

"And how am I going to get in to classes?" she went on. "I'd have to be up at about five-thirty to make it into the city. I wouldn't even be able to get to the station. Buying that house would mean buying a second car or my quitting one semester away from my Master's."

He looked at her, saying nothing.

"That's what you *want*!" she accused, anger welling up. "That's *just* what you want! To trap me in that house with no means of getting around. To keep me there so you'd know what I was doing every minute of every day! You *can't* want that!"

"I can't afford a second car and a mortgage," he said slyly.

"Then we won't buy it!"

"We're buying that house!"

"Paul," she said, trying another tack, "how would I do the grocery shopping? How would I do *anything*? That house is over three miles from the shopping center. It's miles out of the actual town. There aren't any buses. It'd mean waiting until you got home so I could shop at night. Or on weekends."

"Other women manage."

"I'm not *other women*. I'm me. I hate the idea of being so cut off from everything. I hate that house. You can't want to make me a prisoner that way."

"You'll have to learn to live with it. I am going to buy that house." He had an odd, mounting sense of déjà vu; the almost stifling sensation that all of this had happened before. But he'd been on the receiving end then. This time he'd maintain the upper hand.

"*Paul*! How can you want to do something that's wrong

for both of us in every conceivable way? We can't afford that house. We can't afford a second car. The commuting alone would cost you an extra sixty-something dollars a month. And that's only for you. Add me and double it. It's just no good. Can't you *see* that?"

He turned away and went to the kitchen to fix himself a drink.

Exasperated, she followed him.

"*Talk* to me!" she begged. "You're making a completely unilateral decision. That's not what a marriage is supposed to be."

"The longer you continue your education, the fancier your vocabulary becomes," he observed scathingly. "Any day now, I'll be too low-class altogether for you."

"You're not at all low-class. Why do you have to put yourself down every time we talk about my studies? It's some kind of reverse psychology, trying to put me on the defensive, backing me into a corner, making me feel guilty. Paul, I love you. But you want more. You want something I don't think I can give you. I don't think *anyone* can give you what you're after. Because you don't *know* what you want. You're just acting blindly, without any real thought."

"I'd like you to shut up," he said, lifting his glass, then setting it down again. "All the way down the line it's been your show. Now we're going to do something for me."

"This is for you all right. *All* for you. And I'm supposed to tag along like some sort of bonded slave and suffer in willing silence."

"How do you see it as suffering? How do you get to that, eh? Buying a house in a first-class neighborhood, in a first-class town. Eventually, I'll be able to swing another car. I'm due for a promotion in a few more months."

"You just don't see it," she said, shaking her head. "It's crazy. I don't know how to get through to you anymore. Maybe I never did. I can't seem to make you see that buying this house will set us back years. Years! We'll be living and working to pay for a place that's wrong. Just wrong."

"Not 'we'," he said sharply. "Me! I'm the one working, paying."

"I'm sick of hearing that! You do it all the time: give with one hand, then tell me what it cost you with the other. I'm really sick of it. If you're so overburdened being the bread-winner, I'll drop out and get a job."

"No way!"

"What do you mean 'no way'?" What the hell does that mean?"

"I'm not going to have you blaming me for forcing you to drop out. And my wife doesn't work."

"Are you kidding?" She emitted a short, shocked laugh. "Your *wife* doesn't *work*?"

"That's right!"

"This is insane!" she declared, feeling jittery as if she was arguing with a complete stranger. "Your wife doesn't work," she repeated. "My God, talk about archaic! Where the hell do you *get* ideas like that? If I want to work, I'll work. I'll do anything I want. You don't rule me, Paul. You're not my boss, my manager. You don't order me about, direct my life."

"I'm telling you what to do." He took a long swallow of his drink, then slammed the glass down on the counter. "I'm *telling* you." It was all around him now—that feeling it had happened before, all of it; a replay. But he'd change the outcome this time. He'd come out the winner, victorious. This time he would. No tears, no giving in. Not any more.

One last time, she thought. Once more I'm going to introduce a note of reason into this absurd discussion.

"Listen, Paul, you're not making sense." He was pouring more scotch into his glass. She could feel he wasn't listen-ing to her. "Paul, come on, listen! Let's talk about this calmly, rationally. Please! Can't you see it's not a wise move? Let's wait just a little while longer. If we wait another few months, we're bound to find a house we can afford."

"Wait," he said, "so you can finish out your degree. Wait, so you can keep in with all your lofty academic friendships. Wait, so it can all be *your* way. There's supposed to be a little give and take in a marriage, in case you didn't know it, lady. So far, I've been doing all the giving and you've been doing all the taking."

Is that true? she wondered. Is that the way it's been?

"Maybe that's true," she said gently. "Maybe it is and I just haven't seen it. If it is true, I'm sorry. I never realized you felt that way. I thought things were the way *we both* wanted them. But maybe it is one-directional. Perhaps I should get a job and help out, pay the household expenses, take a little of the pressure off you."

"Did you happen to notice," he said with studied casualness, pausing to finish his drink then top it off again, "how you used the words crazy and insane, calm and rational? Or was it irrational?" He stared at her.

He's getting drunk, she realized, suddenly nervous.

"Don't drink any more," she said, low, placing her hand on the counter over his.

He slapped her hand away. *"First I'm insane. Now I'm a drunk!"* he shouted, his face suffused with color, his temples throbbing visibly "Christ almighty, I'm *up to here* with your self-righteous wisdom and mealy-mouthed truly-sorry shit! Who the *fuck* d'you *think* you *are* anyway?" He could see *her* face, *her* hands; how she looked in that instant before the first blows fell. Not any more. "You'll fucking well do what *I* say!" He glared at her for several seconds, then whacked the glass off the counter. It shattered on the floor, ice cubes skidding over the linoleum, finding hiding places beneath the counters, beside the refrigerator. His fists clenched and he was hitting *her* as hard as he could, repaying *her*, shutting *her* up, showing *her* she couldn't get away with any of that stuff anymore. No more.

Margot ran out of the kitchen and he pursued, trapping her in the bedroom, holding her down, hitting her. Hitting, hitting, as hard as he could. Until his head seemed to clear all at once and he blinked, seeing the blood streaming from her nose, her mouth. She was screaming, had been screaming for some time and he hadn't heard.

"Oh, Christ!" he whispered, aghast. "Margot!" He'd thought … not her … but *her*. But it wasn't *her*. Not *her*.

She lay gazing up at him, her eyes fixed in terror; sobbing, her chest heaving. Her head, her whole body was stitched with pain. She took a sudden deep breath and shoved him away, leaped off the bed and ran to the living room, snatching up her coat and bag. She ran, sobbing, to the elevator and down, out to the street. God, God! What should I do? I can't get on a bus. A taxi. I need a taxi. There was a pay phone in the laundry room. She dashed back into the building and ran down the fire stairs to the basement to telephone for a taxi.

She instructed the operator to have the driver pick her up two blocks away from the building. She didn't want to be anywhere near Paul, near this place. God! His eyes when he'd began hitting her. His eyes had gone as blank and empty as marbles. His lips pulled back to reveal his teeth. Like an animal. She ran along the street, looking up and down for the taxi. It pulled up directly in front of her and she threw open the door as the driver leaned across the front seat asking, "You Mrs. Rayburn?"

"That's right," she gasped, out of breath.

He stared at her and she climbed into the back of the taxi thinking, I must look terrible. The driver's eyes had widened. But he said nothing, turned forward and set off toward the city and her parents' house.

It was hard to breathe. Every time she took a breath something in her side sent a stabbing pain through her lungs. She fumbled in her handbag for her pocket mirror, trying to see her face in the darkened interior of the cab. With trembling fingers, acting mechanically, avoiding thinking, she dabbed at her face with a spit-dampened tissue, then gave up, shoving the mirror and tissue back into her bag, turning to stare sightlessly at the passing buildings.

How can I tell them? What can I say? I was mugged. Tell them I was mugged. But why wouldn't I be at home with Paul? Oh, God! What can I *tell* them?

She felt so ashamed, so deeply, hideously ashamed. She was panic-stricken, desperately trying to think up some plausible lie. Shame. He'd beaten her with his fists. Pounding, flailing fists. Her tears started again and she sat hunched in the corner of the seat, sick with shame, humiliation. Did I provoke him? she asked herself, attempting to go back over it all coherently. Did I? God, *did* I?

Her mother opened the door and turned pale at the sight of her. She lifted her hand, then dropped it, stepping back to open the door wider, her eyes filled with horror. Without a word, she led Margot upstairs and into her old bedroom. With her lower lip caught between her teeth, Ingrid began undressing her. Numbly, stunned, Margot watched her mother's face; lifting her arms, shifting her legs, allowing herself to be stripped like an obedient child.

Ingrid went into the bathroom and returned carrying a basin of water and a sponge.

"Lie down," Ingrid said, perching on the side of the bed with the basin in her lap, starting to clean Margot's face. "Why did he do it?" she asked softly, her eyes following her hands as she squeezed the sponge into the water.

"How do you know who did it?" Margot asked, alarmed.

"Why?" Ingrid repeated, ignoring the question. "Tell me why. Tell me what kind of man does this!"

"I don't *know* why," she whispered, tears seeping down the sides of her face, further humiliated by her mother's instant knowledge, her intelligent, intuitive guesswork. "Please, don't tell anyone. I'm so *ashamed*."

Ingrid tried to assemble her many thoughts, her several reactions. "Is this the first time?" she asked, finally.

Margot closed her eyes, turning her head away.

"You think you will make it go away by pretending it did-n't happen? If you do not talk about it, it isn't real? Talk about it! Tell me! This is what I'm here for."

"I can't!" Margot wailed. "I *can't*."

Ingrid dropped the sponge into the basin, setting the basin down on the night table. "I have been watching this happen," she said, sounding resigned, sad. "I had hoped you had more self-respect, more intelligence. It hurts you to breathe?"

"My ribs ..."

"I will call the doctor."

"Mama, no!"

"Don't be a fool!" Ingrid said sharply. "I cannot fix your injuries. I am not a doctor."

Her mother's anger surprised her. She'd expected sympa-thy, not this icy, outraged anger.

"I love you," Ingrid softened her voice. "I love you. But you are a *fool*." She got up and went out to telephone the family doctor.

Margot closed her eyes and sobbed, wanting to die. Too many people were going to know what Paul had done to her. She wanted so badly to die, wished it was something that could be accomplished just by wanting it strongly enough. She tried carefully to hold her mind away from Paul, away from the picture of the animal madness that had transformed his entire face. He'd been someone utterly unrecognizable to her for those long minutes as his fists collided with her head and body, as his breath rattled between his teeth and sweat sprang up all over his body. He hadn't even smelled like Paul. He'd given off a rancid, unhealthy odor; like something that had died beneath the floorboards and was in the process of rotting, its malevolent stench pervading the entire house. Don't think about it! she warned herself.

She opened her eyes and looked around the familiar room, once again wishing she'd never gone to Suzanne's party, had never met him. Yet, remembering, she felt herself softening, swaying toward him. They'd had so much fun, so many good times.

How could you do this to me? How could you when I love you, when I've defended you to *everyone?* She cried harder, thinking of how much effort she'd put into loving him. Her love for him was like the most serious of her injuries, pain radiating out from its core. I love you. You tried to kill me, beat me to death. If I did provoke you, I swear I don't know how. Or why. I love you. Why did you do this to me? How *could* you? I wish you had killed me now. It'd be better than having my own mother stand over me with pain frozen in her eyes, calling me a fool. The shame. God, how you've shamed me! Made me a fool in my mother's eyes. Why, why?

Six

T HE DOCTOR TAPED UP HER RIBS AND PUT TWO sutures in her lip, all the while looking as if there was a great deal he was anxious to say but determined not to say any of it.

After he'd gone, Ingrid came in and stood for a long time staring at her. Margot found it insufferable having her mother look at her that way; knowing her mother had to see her as pathetic, despicable. She'd managed to get herself beaten. There had to have been something she'd done to bring this on herself. Her mother's face held the same expression the doctor's had.

"It's late," Ingrid said at last, wondering if Margot would seek to avail herself of the opening she'd given her earlier.

"I'm sorry," Margot said. It *was* late and her mother looked tired. "I didn't think … I mean, there wasn't anywhere else I could go."

"This will always be your home. I must be up early in the morning, so I will say good night."

"All right."

Talk to me! Ingrid prayed. Open your mouth and ask for help, ask for something. Don't simply accept this! You have never been weak or dishonest with us. Don't begin now! Say something! She stood a moment longer hoping Margot would speak. But she didn't.

"Good night." Ingrid bent to press her lips to Margot's forehead.

She turned her face away, hearing her mother straighten and draw a wearied sigh before quietly going out, closing the door behind her. Margot turned off the light and lay staring into the darkness.

Paul. She curled into herself, trembling. How had this happened? And why couldn't they talk, discuss things sanely, peacefully? Everything she said seemed to trigger his anger. Everything *he* said seemed pointed toward forcing her into saying those things that would detonate his anger. Like a circle. Beginning with him. Ending with him. It has to stop! We can't keep on this way. We've got to sit down together and talk. Talk about this marriage and what's happening to it. We have to reach an agreement. I have to make you see you can't do the things you do. Make you *see*.

She was convinced she could find a way to reason with him, bring him to awareness of himself. She couldn't believe there wasn't a route available to the inside of Paul's logic. She could change him, help him understand himself and, in the process, make him see how his actions were affecting her. She refused to believe he'd meant to do the things he'd done. Striking her, beating her. He'd done it because she'd unwittingly uttered a combination of remarks that had backed him into a corner. I must never again refer to his mother. Never. I have to stop setting up my parents as an example. I have to stop using words like crazy, irrational, calm. My God! It's impossible. I can't do all that.

She felt most injured not by the fact that he'd beaten her but by the fact that he *could*. The Paul she knew and loved simply wasn't capable of that kind of cold-blooded violence. Something hidden, something dangerous caused him to do those things. He couldn't help himself. He had so few outlets for his energies and his abilities. He talked frequently about how limited his scope was in his present position at the office, how much happier he'd feel given a little more administrative mobility. He needed his chances just as she needed hers.

You love me. I know you love me. And I love you. I do. You don't, I know you don't want to be without me. We can keep this marriage going. I won't give up. We can talk it out, settle it. I'll make you see that if you don't get yourself under control, everything we have will be destroyed.

But he'd wanted to kill her, would have killed her if something hadn't stopped him. She'd seen it happen, seen his eyes lose their sick opacity and suddenly assume an expression of stark horror as his hands fell away from her and his body started to tremble. He'd come back to himself as visibly as he'd departed—in the interim having been replaced by someone neither of them knew.

We can work this out. I'm positive we can. I won't give up so easily.

Yet inside, deep inside, she was terrified. Of him. Of his doing it all again.

✠   ✠   ✠

In the morning, early, having been awake all night, she dressed and quietly left the house. She simply couldn't face the morning and her mother and father, the expressions in their eyes, their questions. She had to show them she could solve her own problems, handle situations with some degree of maturity.

Paul was asleep, fully dressed, looking as if he'd fallen in the precise spot he'd been in when she'd run out. Standing beside the bed looking down at him she was overcome by sorrow for him and hopelessness for the situation. Despair gripped her throat, choking her. Pity for this thirty-two-year-old man looking like a small boy, his outflung, sleep-heavy limbs strewn across the bed; dark blood spatters dried on his shirt. Look at you, she thought, sleeping in my blood. What kind of man *are* you after all?

She silently moved away and lay down on the sofa with a blanket. Chilled. Tired and bruised. She shivered once, violently, then felt her body begin manufacturing warmth, and shut her eyes, plummeting into an exhausted sleep.

She awakened to find him on his knees beside the sofa, his head pressing uncomfortably into her mid-section, making agonized sounds. His tears, the way his body shook, grieved her. How had the two of them come to this? She put her hand on the back of his head and at the contact his arms fastened around her, apologies streaming from his mouth.

"I'm sorry, I'm sorry. Forgive me. Please, my God, I can't stand it! Tell me you forgive me! I didn't mean to do it. You're the only one in the world who means anything to me, Margot. Everything. You're all I've got. *Please!*"

She listened, feeling removed, feeling aged and depleted; but convinced, still, they could talk this out. She interpreted his words and actions now as hopeful signs.

He lifted his head and gingerly touched his hand to her face, whispering, "Christ almighty! Look what I did to you! Don't hate me! I'm sorry, *sorry!* Tell me what to do, what you want me to do. I swear to you I'll do it. Anything."

This was what she wanted to hear. But she had to shake her head negatively. She suddenly had no idea what to tell him, what she wanted him to do. She could only hold him, stroking him as he hid his face against her breasts and cried like the little boy he'd appeared to be when she'd stood watching him sleep.

After a time, he raised himself and smiled tearfully, expectantly into her face, sensing she'd forgiven him.

"I'll take a shower, make breakfast," he proposed, his eyes pleading with her to accept this small peace offering.

"All right," she said, in a voice that sounded elderly, ragged.

She watched him go into the bathroom, listened to the sound of the shower being started, unable for the moment to move from where she was. Her face hurt miserably, felt swollen to twice its size. The tape binding her ribs seemed to be forcing the pain inward so that each breath she drew was accompanied by a grimace. She heard the shower being turned off and a minute later he appeared in the doorway, tying the belt of his robe.

"I'll stay home today," he said quietly, looking almost indecently clean, scrubbed; his features chastened, humbled. As if the shower had been a sanctified purification ritual.

"Yes," she said, stiffly pushing off the blanket and sitting up.

"You do forgive me, don't you?" he asked, watching her as if he expected her to topple over.

"I don't know. I can't think."

She got up and went into the bathroom. The thought of food sickened her. She deposited her clothes in the hamper, then crawled into bed, pulling the blankets close around her, shivering again. It occurred to her she was going to miss two key classes today. But what did it matter? She tucked her hands between her thighs for warmth, aware of Paul watching her from the doorway.

"Don't you want breakfast?"

"I'm not hungry."

"I'll get you some coffee," he volunteered eagerly, hurrying off to the kitchen to pour her a cup, carrying it back to the bedroom—leaving a trail of spilled coffee in his wake—to set it down on the night table.

She sat up, adjusting the pillows behind her before reaching for the cup. He stared at the tape wrapped around beneath her breasts, drawing in his breath apprehensively.

"Nothing's broken," she said, looking into her cup. "Just a few cracks."

"I'm sorry," he whispered, unable to stop staring at her breasts sitting neatly above the white bandage. As if she was wearing an exotically contrived garment meant to display her breasts to advantage. Her breasts. He could contain them in his hands, hold them captive like small, pulsing animals; feeling their softness. He approached the bed and sat down beside her, longing to touch her; very aroused.

"Margot?" His voice came out deep, husky with hunger. "I love you," he said, looking deep into her eyes. "I *love* you."

"I know you do," she said softly, setting the coffee cup down. "I know that."

He put his hand on her breast, then leaned toward her, his mouth meeting hers as he reached for her hand, guiding it inside his robe as he bore her down on the pillows, frantically searching her mouth. She didn't want this, yet she did. This was a measure of reassurance on another level and although his weight on her was almost unbearably painful, she bore it, passively accepting his kisses—on her mouth, her breasts—while he seemed to expand inside the circle of her fingers, shuddering suddenly, moaning, "I love you, I love you," as he spilled himself through her fingers.

"I love you," she murmured soothingly, stroking his hair, his fiery face pressed to her breasts. In her other hand he was a new-born starling, small and damp and cold.

✠   ✠   ✠

"We can't pretend it didn't happen. We have to talk about it, Paul."

"I know, I know. I've withdrawn my bid on the house. You were right about that. It just seemed so important. But you were right."

"I'm not talking just about the house. I'm talking about *what happened.* How could you do that? Why? I don't understand how you could do that."

"I didn't *know* I was going to do that. I didn't even know what … was happening. Then all of a sudden … it just …"

"You can't let yourself lose control that way," she said, feeling very much in control now herself. They were headed in the right direction. "You can see that, can't you? You can see how important it is that we discuss things quietly, talk everything out?"

"You're right. You are. You're right."

Why didn't it *sound* the way it should have? The words were all there. But the tone … something was missing.

"You *do* see, don't you Paul? Look at me. Do you?"

"It'll never happen again. I swear to you it won't. I had too much to drink. That's it," he said earnestly, positive he'd found a justifiable reason. "And," he went on quickly, "we'll find something we can afford so that you can keep on with your classes. Whatever you want, anything. We'll do whatever you want."

"It isn't just what I want. That *is* one-directional. I don't want a marriage like that. What's important is what's good for both of us. I'm not trying to deprive you of things you want. But we have to stay in touch with each other, *listen* to what we each have to say. Because if you ever hit me again, I'll leave you and I won't come back. I mean it, Paul. I love you. But if it ever happens again, I'll leave for good."

"Everything'll be okay now, Louis. I swear, kid."

"Don't be funny now, Paul," she warned gently. "Not now."

"You're right," he said, instantly sobered. "Just don't leave me. I'd die."

"I'm tired," she said, her body twitching with the need to rest.

"Sleep," he encouraged. "Go to sleep."

He sat in the living room eating the now-cold breakfast he'd cooked, looking out at the early morning glare of sunlight on the lake. He ate fast, ravenously hungry, then sat back savoring a cup of reheated coffee and a cigarette, recalling something that made him feel momentarily frightened, guiltier: the fantastic feeling that had surged through him while it had been happening. It was all he seemed able to remember: the euphoria, the stunning sensations of feeling freer, stronger, more powerful than he ever had. Fists hitting flesh, crashing against bone. He'd been charged, elated, his chest expanding like a bellows with the power that had coursed through his body and poured out through his fists.

Nothing, not even lovemaking, had ever given him such an engulfing, total high. Throughout, he'd been throbbingly erect; deriving the most hotly physical satisfaction from his actions. Yet the recollection made him feel sick now, full of self-hate and shame.

He exhaled, sinking down into the sofa, promising himself he'd never go so far out of control again. Christ almighty! Hitting someone he loved as much as he loved Margot. She was the only one he'd ever loved. Except for *her*. And look what she'd done to him, to his love for her!

Her poor face, what he'd done to her. How could he have done that to Margot? His Margot. She belonged to him. But he'd wanted to kill her, to hit and keep on hitting her until she was dead. And then he'd have won.

Well, it was all over now. Behind them. He'd buy her something, he thought, warming to the idea. They'd go out more. He'd be nicer to her parents. Her parents. He sat upright, chilled. That's where she'd gone. Until that moment, he hadn't given any thought to where she'd gone. She'd run home. So they knew what'd happened, knew what he'd done to her. Christ almighty! Why hadn't he stopped her? He shouldn't have let her go running out that way. But he'd been so shocked, so immobilized, realizing what had happened, that he'd been completely unable to move or think. And by the time his brain had started working again, it'd been too late. She'd gone. Home. To her mother and father. Damn them! Now they'd have something new to hold over his head. It'd show in their eyes, in the way they'd talk to him from now on. Christ! He should've stopped her.

But maybe she'd lied, made up some story. Something. Margot wouldn't give him away, running home like a kid to blurt out what had been done to her. She wasn't like that. She could handle herself. She could've told them anything. No! He shook his head angrily. She'd told them. That was a professional bandaging job. And the tape on her lip. That meant those two interfering sons-of-bitches had brought in a doctor. Christ! He was hot now, sweating. Three people who knew he'd beaten her. Who else? If she'd gone on the bus ... No, no. A cab. She wouldn't have gone on a bus looking like that. So there was a cab driver who'd seen her too. Four people. It was stacking up. He felt panicked. Witnesses. People who knew he was someone who used his fists on his wife. I'll *kill* her if she told them. No, no! Don't think that way! Think! This is Margot, my wife. She wouldn't betray me. Not Margot, not her. My baby, my Margot. She loves me. Didn't she just do that for me ... Didn't she just ... Not my Margot. She'd never let me down.

I'll get us a house. But something smaller. She's right about that. That place was too big, too expensive. I'll find the perfect place, surprise her. Get another car too. That raise is just about in my pocket. With that, I'll be up to twenty-four. If those bastards don't fuck me around. They'd better not fuck around with me! They wouldn't dare give that promotion to anyone else. That's mine.

Tomorrow. I'll start looking tomorrow. I don't have to

drag her around with me. I can find the place by myself.
Surprise her with it.

He sat back once more, letting his head rest against the
sofa, his eyes half-closed as he visualized the two of them
in their house, two cars in the driveway. Six more weeks
and she'd be finished with her degree. Then she'd stay at
home where she belonged, fixing the place up, shopping,
doing the things a wife's supposed to do. Getting the meals,
putting up curtains.

He could see himself climbing down from the commuter
train, saying good-bye to the other men—smiles and
see-you-in-the-morning—walking across the lot to pick up
the car, driving toward home; pulling into the driveway,
hearing the satisfying *chuk* of the car door as it slammed
shut. On the way up the walk to his front door and his wife
waiting, looking and smelling good, maybe hot, they'd
make it before dinner, then laugh and eat half-naked in
front of the fireplace. Good. It'd be good. He could see her
listening, paying close attention as he told her about his
day in town, about business. He could *see* it.

✠   ✠   ✠

She dreamed she was suspended from the ceiling of a dank,
torch-lit underground cavern. By chains around her wrists
and ankles. Forced to face forward, her shoulders pulled
halfway out of their sockets by the chains. Her legs spread
wide. There were half a dozen other women similarly suspended, their faces empty, expressionless, resigned. It's a
dream, she told herself, twisting her head to look around
her. The smell of the place was sickening. Mold and dark,
wet things. And the heat was suffocating. Sweat was trick-
ling from her armpits, dropping from her body. The bodies
of the other women looked shiny, golden in the flickering
light.

As she watched, two men came into the chamber carrying whips coiled around their hands. They were smiling, their eyes glinting with evil. They stopped in front of one of the women nearest the door. The smaller of the two men grabbed at the woman's breasts, laughing aloud with satisfaction as she seemed to suddenly come to life and attempted to twist her body away from him.

Angry, shouting something unintelligible, the larger of the two men threw his arm around the woman's waist, holding her steady as the smaller man took the handle of his whip, reversed it and with a grunt, rammed it between the woman's legs. Her screams filled the air, echoing echoing, terrorizing Margot. The smaller man withdrew the whip, once more wrapped it around his hand and said something to the other man. The two of them looked in Margot's direction, nodding, then moved slowly down the length of the room.

Her mouth opened but she had no tongue. She shook her head violently, begging with her eyes. But the larger man simply laughed and signaled to his friend who casually flicked his hand, causing the whip to uncoil as he stepped forward from the shadows. Noiselessly, she screamed and screamed, her throat working as the smaller man ran his hand casually up her thighs. Her head snapped back, her eyes bulging, the cords in her neck standing out, as recognition and Paul's whip handle came to her simultaneously.

Seven

WITHIN A WEEK, HE FOUND AND BOUGHT A HOUSE IN
that same town. He was in love with the place, its quaint-
modern mix of shops, its meticulously landscaped houses,
its aura of money and success. He was also in love with the
house.

Three bedrooms, two full bathrooms, a huge kitchen,
paneled dining room, French-doored living room and
attached two-car garage, on one half-acre of land he had
great plans for landscaping. Maybe they'd go all the way
and have an in-ground swimming pool too.

He was brimming with plans, excitement. Ideas darted
through his brain like hornets, pausing to stab him every so
often, directing him this way and that. Exuberant over his
promotion and accompanying raise, he expansively ushered Margot into a Ford dealership where he bought her a
two-year old Mustang in not-too-bad condition. She
accepted it with an initial uncertainty that soon departed
as she began enjoying her new mobility and the illusion of
freedom the car provided.

She finished her thesis and turned to attending to the
house, finding herself with little free time in which to
mourn the ending of her academic life. The house, with its
near-empty rooms, demanded attention, and she felt obli-
gated to live up to her expected role in this venture. So she

began attempting to furnish and decorate these rooms, many of which might remain empty unless they magically re-established financial solvency and could begin having children. Of course, after discussing it, they were both forced to agree children would have to wait at least two more years. She didn't mind. She had the decided feeling children were not a good idea just yet. Paul, although he cloaked his feelings in logistics, patently had no intention of sharing her with a baby.

She did want a child, and daydreamed frequently about having one, but fear invariably accompanied her daydreams. Fear specifically of Paul's temper and a vague fear of childbearing itself. She'd become reluctant to approach anything that carried with it the possibility of pain. She couldn't watch police shows on television, or those private investigator shows. Anything with the likelihood of at least one scene being a violent episode. Even the six o'clock news, which included the goriest possible details and a lot of local violence. She ignored the morning papers, paid close attention to whatever book she might be reading in the evening while Paul watched television. It seemed as if she was walking around holding her breath, treading very carefully even when alone.

When faced with the empty walls and expanses of hardwood floor, she felt further defeated; she'd never possibly be able to take these rooms and translate them into a home. The kitchen, with all the new, color-coordinated appliances Paul had insisted upon, struck her as possessing the same sterile charm as an operating room. The butcherblock counters flanking the stainless steel sink made her think of an abattoir and she simply couldn't get that image out of her mind. So she avoided that counter and did her cutting and chopping on a small, square board she purchased at Noah's Ark in town.

Noah's Ark was a shop she stopped in almost every time

she went into town. She'd walk up and down the aisles, cir-
cling the displays, enjoying the look of cast-iron pots,
Scandinavian dishes, multicolored mugs, wooden utensils;
plant-hangers, baskets of rope and wicker, pot-racks, oven
mitts. Anything that might turn that stainless steel kitchen
into someplace cozy and inviting.

She carried home armloads of knick-knackery, setting out
her bright orange mugs and baskets of dried flowers, only to
step back in dismay, seeing her efforts had in no way
altered the starkly sterile room with its surfaces of wood
and shining steel. Nothing seemed decorative or eye-
catching enough to draw her attention away from the
light-reflections on the dishwasher door, the refrigerator
door, the stove door, the sink. Stainless steel coldly defying
her attempts to make it warm.

Their bedroom, with the exception of new curtains and
installed carpeting, was a replica of their bedroom in the
old apartment. The same furniture distributed in the same
way, but looking miniaturized in the huge master bedroom
with its fireplace, its separate dressing room and its adjoin-
ing bathroom complete with two sinks, toilet, bidet, shower stall, tub and built-in linen-towel closet. When she was
in this bathroom, her breathing seemed to bounce back at
her from the walls and ceilings, giving her the feeling the
door might not open when she turned the knob and might
trap her inside. She began leaving the bathroom door
open.

The house abounded in fireplaces. Five of them. All in
need of cleaning, the chimneys requiring pointing. And
the first time it rained, water streaks appeared on the bedroom ceiling. The shingles were rotting and needed to be
replaced.

For a week, men crawled around on the roof; some of
them at work on the chimneys, others hammering down
the new roofing. She was glad of their noisy presence and

offered coffee and fresh-baked brown bread; delighting in their preoccupied, muted conversations as they politely accepted and ate her offerings before returning to their duties on the roof.

After the workmen left for good, she felt desperately lonely. She missed their noise and their good manners. Their deferential politeness had surprised her. They'd been well-spoken, clean and considerate, shattering whatever preconceived notions she'd had that laborers were laborers because they were unsuited to the professional world, because they lacked education or motivation or family money. She was mortified by her stereotypical preconceptions and vowed never again to make assumptions about people purely on the basis of their occupations. Even the man who collected the garbage was quiet, friendly, polite and, again, well-spoken. Was it this town? she wondered. She believed it was. The people here demanded a high level of quality in all areas, including service-related ones. The only black she saw was the light-skinned man who drove the garbage truck. Occasionally she saw women who were obviously daily help waiting quietly by the road to be picked up and taken home. But the town itself seemed to have no black residents. She saw none in the supermarkets, none in the shops, none in the streets in town. Their absence, to her, was conspicuous and intentional. It gave her the feeling she was black and in this town under false pretenses.

As she wandered, pen and paper in hand, through the rooms, she realized she had, in the years of her marriage to Paul, absorbed a great number of prejudices as a result of simply listening to him. Now she was engaged in the process of actively disencumbering herself of these. I've got a good mind of my own, she told herself, studying the blank walls; I must use it. I can't allow myself to become an appendage, an extension of Paul. She was coming to view the majority of his opinions and preferences as decidedly juvenile, influenced by remarks he'd heard other people make, not experiences he'd directly undergone. She was surprised not to have seen this sooner. But she was definitely seeing it now.

Life with Paul continued to be unnaturally quiet. She felt suspicious, on the alert, and mildly, permanently agitated. It was as if a truce had been declared, and they were merely settled in the lull of tense preparedness between battles. Yet he seemed changed. He came home smiling. Tired and filled with happy-sounding complaints about the commuter trains, comments about his fellow commuters, anecdotes. The trains were crowded, overheated or not heated at all. There was no place to sit half the time because there were too many loud jokers taking up extra seats so they could continue their running bridge-gin-poker game that began in the morning and ended on the return trip. He complained of these things and more, but his face showed he relished being one of the ranks of that brigade of trim-suited men with attaché cases and duplicated reports making their way into the city. Frequently, when she picked him up at the station—the old Thunderbird was beginning to sink ungracefully into its dotage—she'd sit in the Mustang and watch him descend from the train, smiling and bidding good night to half a dozen other men who all looked identical; smiling, looking so pleased and self-satisfied. He'd climb into the car and kiss her passionately as if his contact with these men stoked his lust, fired his sensuality. She felt daily more uneasy, removed both from him and his life away from her; unable to connect with or comprehend the pleasure he was obviously deriving from the men, the town, the house and the life they were living.

His demands sexually were as urgent and sustained as before, even more so. But she was having more and more trouble responding to him. It took him longer to stimulate her, longer to make her come. And she was enduring these acts rather than enjoying them. She performed her role but let her mind wander elsewhere as she suffered his weight and his thrusting presence inside her. He spread her this way or turned her that way, and she went where she was directed, feeling very little, not even involved. She found his flushed, straining urgency a little pathetic and watched the two of them—the rider and his accommodating mount—from a distance, secretly deriding the act and the man. She was coming to dislike lovemaking and chanced the occasional lie in order to extricate herself from her nightly, expected compliance. Headaches, the start of her period. Just occasionally, so that she might for one night sleep soundly, undisturbed and unchafed.

At some moments, when she saw his mouth opening avidly, his tongue extending toward her body, she despised him so totally that she had to close her eyes in order not to watch what he did. If she watched, she might actually say or do something. And, one action leading to another, he might in turn seek to do her harm.

Gradually, the rooms filled with furniture. She masked her disinterest in approval of Paul's selections, going along with him on Saturday afternoon shopping trips to browse through furniture stores, selecting a chair here, a lamp there, writing out checks or sliding his credit card across counters with the air of a contented man, well satisfied with his selections. He *was* happy, she saw, studying the definition of his boyish profile as he signed a charge slip or wrote out a check. How, she asked herself, can acquiring all these things make you so happy? The small things she bought she spent far too much time deliberating about, and they gave her little if any satisfaction.

As she prowled the rooms of the house or wandered back and forth across the lawn at the rear of the house, she felt something, a knowledge flirting closer and closer to her. She'd stop and stand very still, willing it to come to her. Her mind would expand receptively as she held herself poised and open. But it refused to come.

The only breaks came on her Sunday visits home. Her parents made the drive out to see them only once. It had n't been a successful visit. Perhaps because she felt so out-side of all of it: the house, the town, her husband. On that day, she failed even to connect with her mother and father. Tacitly, it was agreed the Sunday visits would continue as before. So after browsing lazily through the Sunday papers, they'd tidy up, put on Sunday-casual clothes and drive into the city in the slowly decaying Thunderbird.

On those drives into the city she felt decidedly odd. This oddness struck her with regularity each Sunday as Paul took the Thunderbird flying—making it shudder and rat-tle—along the Old Shore Expressway into the city. She'd look out to see new high-rise buildings on the way up, to see the gray wash of the polluted incoming tide foaming against the shore, to see the modifications and improve-ments being made to the lake front and to feel that every-thing around her was moving on, progressing, changing while she remained static, unchanged. Caught, trapped. Suspended inside herself, her house, and her marriage.

The marriage now held long silences. While Paul changed out of his "city" clothes, she worked in the kitchen readying dinner. They would eat in relative silence. Then she'd tidy the kitchen—they rarely used the dining room—load the dishwasher, slam its stainless steel door as if she'd managed to trap a rabid animal inside, press the starter button and stand listening to the first rush of water through the machine before going out to join Paul in the living room where he was already engaged in reading the evening paper while the news was delivered to them through their new Japanese color television set.

She'd sit with a book in her lap and forget to read, spending her time covertly studying Paul or else gazing without listening at the marvelous color of the television set. Sometimes, giving in to a desperate need to break the silence, to escape from herself, she'd cross the room to sit on his lap in an attempt to find in this man someone she recognized. Always pleased by these displays, he'd work his hand up under her dress if she was wearing one, or down the top of her shirt if she was in trousers, and she'd lie across his lap like a rug as the availability and weight of her body built up his appetite and, in direct ratio, reduced hers. She never received from him what she'd gone forward expecting.

Uneasy at her own perversity, divorced from their bodies' activities, she'd lie on the floor or the sofa or in their bed and quiver responsively, convulsively as she watched herself make love with him. She'd notice the way his hands crept possessively over her breasts or thighs, the way his face looked as he put himself inside her. He remained unrecognizable. She did wonder if she appeared equally unfamiliar to him. Again demonstrating her new perversity, she'd enjoy these random, naked encounters; deriving an abandoned, whorish-feeling pleasure from his manipulations.

This whorish feeling led her into a variety of speculations while he delved in the depths of her body. Could I make love with anyone? Would it feel any differently if I did? Does it matter to me that it's you? Or could I lie here and open my thighs to some other man? She had the feeling she possibly could. Because making love with Paul was not only impersonal, it was divorced entirely from anything having to do with her emotions. Impersonal. Routine. The time when she might look at him and feel a delicious, explosive yearning had passed. Now she saw him through harshly critical eyes, noting that his body was changing,

becoming thick through the middle, a rounded belly growing. Like a pregnancy, she thought, fascinated by the way
his flesh trembled at her touch. His neck seemed to be getting thicker too. And his hair was no longer the abundant,
luxurious growth it had been six years earlier. It was thin-
ner, less springy. He didn't look much older than he had six
years before. His face still held that boyish charm, that
look of incipient mischief-making. But his comedy routines had disappeared from his repertoire. On the occasional Saturday night when they went out to dinner and he
had half a dozen or so drinks before, during and after dinner, the routines came back. But otherwise, he'd abandoned them. She missed them.

Now that he was no longer given to sudden changes of
voice and character, she realized she'd been terribly
attracted to him because of them. She'd liked the sudden
switches, the dialects he'd done so cleverly. She'd liked the
shine to his eyes and the heat of his body when, finding her
a good audience, he'd warmed to the task, creating outra-
geously funny dialogues. He couldn't perform, she now saw,
without an audience. And she'd ceased applauding, could-
n't return to being that appreciative, willing girl. She
mourned her passing and was lonely for the two other people they'd been at the beginning.

Paul, she believed, had finally found his full-time role:
that of the successful, upwardly mobile young executive,
playing house for keeps with the attractive, well-built,
blonde robot disguised as his wife. She felt she'd go mad
spending day after day alone in the house with nothing
beyond bed-making, laundry and the preparation of meals
to occupy her. She saw herself slowly evolving into a "sub-
urban housewife" and was panicked by the image. So she
started spending her afternoons in town, idly browsing
through the shops, trying, as she picked things up and then
put them down, to align her thoughts.

What's happened to me? she wondered, feeling the onset of panic. I'm getting older, but my life feels as if it's stopped. There's nothing I need. Things, I don't need things. Paul needs things. I need people. Where are all the people, the friends, the ones to talk with? Alone. All by myself. Alone even with Paul in the evenings. More alone with him. The weekends. Sunday, one day a week when I'm alive and I drag my mind out of mothballs and try to get it started. Six other days when all I can see, think, feel is loneliness, boredom. Unable to fight off the boredom. There are only just so many hours I can spend reading, cooking, cleaning. Those hours are used up so quickly, leaving me with empty hands and this dreadful malaise that sends me out to the car and into town to walk up and down the aisles of one store after another, rarely purchasing anything; just looking, looking, seeing other women who seem to know their purpose, their destination. Or do they? What is it about this town, the people I see that strikes such a jarring note in my mind?

The women all appeared to be interchangeable. Wearing uniforms. Well-cut pant-suits or a particular type of dress, one brand of shoes. The hair cut in one of three prevailing styles. Their voices all one—college-educated, moneyed. Even the children looked bored, bitter and greedy. The girls groaning audibly as the mothers pressed them into uniforms for the young; the boys looking menacing as if they might, with their peachy young faces and oversized hands, pounce upon you in the parking lot and perform savage acts of violence upon your person to retaliate against some unspecified crime. Groups of young boys with ten-speed bikes or, slightly older, with motorcycles. They frightened her with their assessing eyes, sending her hurrying on her way to the safety of some store or the interior of the Mustang to sit, shaky and breathless, wondering why she was frightened. Why? When she could offer herself naked to Paul with an absence of emotion so complete that she guiltily sought to compensate with inventive-sexual performances.

The two of them rarely spoke of love now and she missed hearing him state how much he loved and needed her. The only time she could count on his saying it was after he'd come, half-sobbing, inside her. Then he'd fold down into the circle of her arms, bury his face in her neck and whisper, I love you. Even then she didn't believe that he meant he loved her. She interpreted this I-love-you as meaning, Thank you for letting me come in you. Thank you for letting me touch and lick and explore and fondle you. And, automatically, she said, I love you too. Because, despite the absence of emotion, his hands and mouth did relieve her, did take away some of the tensions and pressures accumulated during days of doing very little. It was bitterly pleasurable having his tongue and teeth, his lips and fingers send her into that small, tight room of orgasms where the door slammed shut with ringing finality and she was locked in alone with herself. Afterward, they'd separate and she'd turn on her side, her back heated by the warmth of his glutted flesh as she dived into sleep with liquid messages slowly making their way down between her thighs en route to a communication with the sheets and mattress pad.

Still, he appeared to her to be satisfied: with her, with every aspect of his life. A vice-president now, he commanded a secretary, a corner office with mahogany desk, sundry underlings and the president's ear. An executive who lunched with other executives and submitted lengthy expense accounts monthly, he received bonuses, regular increases in salary, stock options and gratuities from grateful clients. He played tennis on Saturday mornings at a newly built indoor tennis club in town as well as his one-night-a-week game in the city with his fellow executives. He also sometimes worked too late to make it home, so stayed in town at his club. He'd joined his university club and on those occasions when Margot came into the city on the pretext of shopping to be done, he took her to an expensive lunch in the rooftop restaurant of the club. She'd sit looking at the club silver, the sparkling white club napery, the club members, the wives of the club members; all of it subdued, elegant; listening to the discreet clink of serving dishes being handled by the club staff. Throughout the meal she'd have the feeling she was dreaming this, that it wasn't real but only imagined.

✠   ✠   ✠

On one of her forays through Noah's Ark, she became engaged in conversation with the owner, a woman whose appearance reminded Margot of her mother. Throughout her conversation, she guiltily studied the tall, wide-shoul-dered woman, realizing with an ache inside that she missed being with her mother, missed the frequent telephone con-versations—what had happened to them?—the lunches, the secure strength of shared embraces.

"Listen, instead of just hanging around," the proprietor—named Wilma—offered with an inviting smile, "come on in and I'll put you to work."

"I've got to do something." Margot smiled back. "I really would love to work in a place like this." She looked around the shop, admiring the ever-changing displays, the as-yet unwrapped new stock.

"I can't pay a hell of a lot," Wilma said, "But I'd enjoy having you around. I sure as hell could use a little intelli-gent help around here. These girls are so goddamned dumb I'm amazed they graduated from kindergarten."

Margot leaned on the counter, enjoying what felt like the first real contact she'd made with anyone outside her par-ents in far too long. She liked the look of Wilma, her long brown hair that she wore pulled back and caught at the nape of her neck with a tortoise-shell barrette. She had full, rounded breasts that seem misplaced on her long, leggy body. About forty, with faint creases around her eyes, she had a habit of looking directly into Margot's eyes with the hint of a smile on her mouth. She wore no rings and a mannish wristwatch on a very knobby wrist.

I've been letting my brain die, Margot thought, watching Wilma as she efficiently, pleasantly rang up a woman's purchases. Even if it's only working in a small shop like this, at least I'll have some opportunity to keep my brain tuned up. A destination for each day, a reason for getting out of bed. She returned to the house fired with enthusiasm. She felt better, younger than she had since handing in her thesis. She prepared a special dinner and laid out the dining room table, adding a vase of dried flowers for a touch of color. The room itself was so dark and drab it seemed to suck the color out of any object placed within it.

Paul sensed something the instant he came through the door. She later thought perhaps she shouldn't have rushed so happily to meet him, shouldn't have hugged and kissed him quite so eagerly, or bubbled nearly so effervescently. But she had the arbitrary idea he might actually enter into her mood, share her optimism.

He poured himself a drink, listening soberly.

"I can start right away. Tomorrow. She'll pay me a hundred a week. It's not a lot, I know. But it means we'll be able to cut back on our expenses. I'll pay the housekeeping expenses and we can bank the extra money. It's a great little shop. And you'll like Wilma."

"I don't want you working," he said quietly.

"Oh, Paul, don't be silly! I'm losing my mind sitting here doing nothing every day. It's a job and I'll get paid."

"You're not taking that job." His anger was so immediate and consuming he could barely see. Now, when he'd thought everything was under control, running the way he'd always wanted it, she had to defy him, start trying to change things.

"What do you mean I'm not taking that job? I've already told her I would."

"Then call her up and say you've changed your mind."

"I haven't changed my mind. I *want* that job."

"There's enough for you to do right here," he said, measuring out his words like medicine.

"It takes me about an hour to do this house every day," she said, creating a smile, determined this would be a rational discussion. "Dinner takes no time at all. I can do all of it when I get home from the shop and have dinner ready before you get here."

"With your education you're going to work as a salesgirl," he said disgustedly. "Was that the point of it all? So you could wind up working behind the counter in some woman's store?"

"If you're being serious, I can always get a proper job in the city and commute with you." She couldn't follow the circuitous turns of his logic. "Is that what you'd like?"

"You call that woman and tell her you're not coming, you've changed your mind."

"If I do that, then I'll start looking for a job in the city."

He set down his untasted drink, grabbed her by the upper arm and backhanded her across the face.

"Goddamn it! When I tell you to do something, you *do* it!"

"Paul ..." She tried to pull free, but his hand tightened around her upper arm, his thumb pressing deep into her flesh.

"*Don't argue with me!*" he shouted, hitting her again. She had to do it. Every single time. She couldn't leave him alone. Always at him, never letting him have any peace.

"*Stop it!*" she cried, throwing her arm up over her face trying to protect herself.

He no longer saw or heard her. Filled with murderous rage, sweating, his eyes fixed, he grabbed her other arm and shook her so hard her head bobbed around on her shoulders. Then he began punching. She cried out, trying to evade the blows but they came and came. She couldn't escape them. As it went on, she began to scream, begging the walls, the ceiling. "*Help me! Somebody help me!*" His fist met her eye, blinding her, sending her crashing into the refrigerator, down to the floor. He stood over her, fists clenched, panting. "Home, you bitch. You stay *home!*" Then suddenly he stepped across her and tore out of the room. She lay where she'd fallen, hearing the hum of the refrigerator like the engine of a jet roaring in her ears, hearing the slam of the bedroom door and she started to push herself up, thinking it was over. But it wasn't. Naked, brandishing his belt, he appeared in the kitchen doorway and she shrank back against the wall as he moved closer.

Please God! Save me! Somebody save me! He's going to kill me.

"Paul," she begged. "Please, stop! Don't *Paul!*"

The bitch was always sorry afterward, hugging him, telling him how much she loved him. Bringing men into the house, making the bed bounce against the wall and the noise and when he woke up and called for her she shouted, Go back to sleep! Then in the morning when the men would be gone she'd come down with her mouth all hard and pull him away from the bowl of cereal he'd fixed himself, grabbing him by the hair, tossing him down, kicking, punching.

He tore at her clothes, ripping them off her. She fought back, trying to save herself, her clothes; the protection the dress and her underwear offered.

"DON'T YOU HIT ME, BITCH!" he screamed, hitting her in the nose with his fist. Her mouth, the back of her

throat was filled with blood. She sobbed, screaming hyster-
ically, scrabbling across the floor trying to get away from
him, crying, "*Please*, Paul! *Stop*! Look at what you're
doing!"

He brought the belt down again and again—across her
arms and breasts, her belly, her thighs. Livid welts sprang
up all over her body and he liked the look of them, the
blood. He dropped the belt, seized her legs, tore off her
pants and plunged into her. She screamed. His hands
closed around her throat, slowly strangling her as he
pumped frantically, his face twisted monstrously, grunting
as he moved faster and faster.

She'd die. She knew it. With each thrust, he rammed her
hard against the wall so that her head was being battered.
Her fight completely gone, she went limp, sobbing as he
quivered from head to toe and spurted into her. Then, still
inside her, his eyes closed, he lowered his weight down on
top of her and lay with his head on her shoulder, his hand
tenderly, rhythmically smoothing her bloodied cheek.

Help me! Please, somebody, help me! Oh God!
Somebody *help* me!

✠   ✠   ✠   ✠   ✠

Eight

SHE KEPT WAITING FOR HIM TO RETURN TO HIMSELF AND begin apologizing. It didn't happen. Without another word to her, he installed himself on the sofa in the living room for the night.

Grateful at least to be left alone she got herself into bed and tried to sleep.

In the morning, after Paul had gone, she telephoned Wilma to say she'd changed her mind. Wilma didn't seem at all surprised or upset. "Come see me anyway," she said, sounding as if this sort of thing had happened to her more than once before. "I'm getting kind of used to seeing you around the place."

Margot said she would, then hung up and went into the bathroom to examine her injuries, her feelings. She hadn't done so the night before, convinced that if she had, Paul would have contrived to use this as a reason for beating her further.

She felt paralyzed, frozen with shock as she stared at her red-purple eye with its nearly closed swollen lid, her bruised cheeks and chin, her split, distended lips. There were raised welts—some of them blood encrusted—on her breasts, her arms, her legs. Everywhere. She couldn't seem to find any place on her body he'd missed.

When she was under the shower and applied the soapy

washcloth between her legs, she cried out as the soap bit
into the raw wounds there. I am wounded, she thought.
Damaged. Abused. She bathed herself with careful hands,
wincing as the soap ate into another tender place, then
another.

Having applied antiseptic to the worst of the cuts, she
stood in her robe, her eyes meeting those of her pallid
reflection, and saw undiluted fear gazing back at her. And
from her side of the glass, she demanded of that woman in
the mirror: Are you just going to stay here and let this keep
on happening to you? Are you? The eyes of the woman in
the mirror slid away, hiding themselves beneath bruised
eyelids, deeply ashamed. You can't go on, she argued with
the mirror image. You've got to get out, away from here.
But how? Inside both women rose a tortured cry. *I'm
trapped*! I'm married to him. I don't love him anymore. But
I'm legally tied to him. What can I do?

Think! Why can't I think?

His actions had in some way robbed her of everything but
fear and an intense desire to crawl into some dark place
and hide there. He'd made it impossible for her to leave the
house now until her injuries healed. Why was he doing
these things? And how could he have become so aroused
by beating her? She was most frightened not by the beating
or the rape but by the way he'd rested on top of her afterward, absent-mindedly caressing her with such deceivingly
gentle hands. As if he'd been rewarding her for being his
victim. Mad. He was mad. The man she'd married was
gone, lost somewhere inside himself. For good, it seemed.
This rapist, this fist-flinging madman had come to take up
permanent residence inside the body that had once been
Paul's.

It was impossible for her to go anywhere looking the way
she did. People would take one look at her and know what
had happened. She'd have to wait. But as soon as the bruis-

es faded, as soon as her strength returned, she'd go. Somewhere. As far from him as she could get. Somewhere he'd never find her.

And now that the idea of escape had come to her, she mourned the expenses of her Master's. With that money, she might have been able to establish herself somewhere safely. There was less than twelve hundred dollars left of her lifetime's savings. But it didn't matter. She'd take what she had and get out, start her life all over again. Clean.

He behaved as if she looked exactly as always, as if nothing out of the ordinary had occurred. He rattled on, smiling, that next evening, about goings-on at the office; drank his two pre-dinner Beefeater martinis, ate the dinner she'd prepared and complimented her heartily on the food, then retired to the living room and the network news with his evening paper.

Stunned, confounded, she cleared the table, started the dishwasher, then quietly seated herself on the sofa in the living room wondering if it wasn't she who'd gone mad. Had she not had the proof: the bruises, the vaginal pain, she might have doubted the events of the night before had actually happened. But faced with his bright, still-mischievous, youthful features as he smoked a cigarette and watched the news, she felt she'd stepped beyond the boundaries of reason into an area of bizarre irrationality. Only his eyes gave any indication of the change in the man. They remained opaque, distant, yet watchful.

One of them was mad. Seriously emotionally ill. His present behavior would have led any outsider to believe she was the sick one, not him. Standing outside herself, looking in as she'd done before the mirror that morning, she believed she had to look deranged, sitting huddled in a corner of the sofa, suspiciously eyeing him. He looked to her like a rampaging tiger, momentarily sated after the kill. His appetite would soon return and then he'd kill again. She was tensely, sweatily waiting.

He made no reference to what he'd done—she guessed that he wouldn't now—and readied himself for bed like an athlete in training. A good boy, following the coach's orders. He showered, brushed his teeth, patted bath powder over his feet and under his arms, then climbed between the sheets with a healthy yawn, appearing quite happy as he watched her pull on a nightgown. He failed even to remark upon the nightgown—a garment she usually wore only when ill—and leaned over to kiss her good night, disregarding the way she flinched. He turned off the light and dropped into sleep with the ease and clear-mindedness of a child.

She lay in the darkness listening to the regular ebb and flow of his breathing, again caught up in that disoriented feeling. It isn't me, she told herself. I'm not crazy. But he'll drive me crazy if I don't make an effort to defend myself.

She assumed they wouldn't be seeing her parents that Sunday. She despaired of the idea of having them see her in her present condition: her face yellow-green with the fading bruises, and thin because she hadn't been able to eat for four days. She'd lost her appetite altogether and had sustained herself on coffee and instant chicken broth. She wanted heat, had a constant desire to put warm liquids inside her. The liquids, however, ran right through her, adding diarrhea to her physical distress. Her entire bottom felt burned, stripped raw. But she needed the coffee, the broth. Something to ease the chill inside. She felt she was slowly turning to ice from the inside out.

Sunday morning, Paul said, "Come on. You'd better start getting dressed. We're going to be late."

She looked up at him. "For what?"

"To your parents' house," he said, looking innocent.

"We're not going today," she said quietly. I won't have them see me this way.

With that same innocent expression, he grabbed her arm, wrenched it up behind her and held it there as he pleasantly said, "Get dressed, Margot. Or we'll be late."

Her eyes filled with tears from the pain, she nodded. He released her. She went to get dressed. As she pulled on trousers—dully noting that they hung around her middle—and a sweater, she understood that Paul wanted her parents to see her this way, wanted them to know what he'd done. Why? How could he want my mother and father to see and know what was happening? In some demented fashion he was trying to display to them tangible proof of his power. That was part of it. The other part was to punish and keep on punishing her. For something she'd done but didn't know about. Maybe just for simply being alive. She applied blue eye shadow to camouflage the bruises, thick cover-up beneath her eyes and along her jaw, some blusher. She looked garish, clown-like.

She knew she would remember for as long as she lived the look on her parents' faces as she and Paul came through the door that day. Her mother quickly reassembled her features into a smile. But her father's mouth opened, then closed tightly, his eyes containing a murderous light as he looked first at her and then at Paul before saying hello in a barely-controlled voice. He stood staring at Paul for a moment, then turned and continued on his way out to the garden, his hand clenched so tightly around the trowel that the ridged impressions from the handle remained imbedded in his palm for hours afterward.

Paul, very sure of himself, settled in the living room with the newspaper while Margot awkwardly sat down at the kitchen table with her mother. Lost for words. She knew if she said anything, she'd say everything. She hated the idea of her mother knowing what her life had become.

Ingrid related a conversation she'd had the previous evening with Suzanne's mother, her eyes never leaving

Margot's face. She kept talking as she opened the refrigerator door and in a surprised tone Margot at once realized was purely for Paul's benefit, said, "No chives. Damn!" She looked at her wristwatch, then meaningfully at Margot and in the same light voice said, "Come on! Hurry! We've just got time to make it to the market before it closes."

Margot snatched up her handbag, quickly donned her sunglasses and followed her mother down the hall.

"We'll be back in half an hour," Ingrid called out. "Help yourself to coffee."

That smoothly, that easily, and they were out. Margot felt she'd just been airlifted out of occupied territory. Ingrid said nothing until they were well away from the house. She drove the short distance to Remington Park, stopped the car and turned on the seat to look at Margot.

"What is happening?" she asked, allowing her feelings to surface on her face, in her voice.

Margot looked at her, opened her mouth to speak, couldn't, and fell sobbing into her mother's arms.

"What will you do?" Ingrid asked, holding her, determined not to interfere or give advice unless it was asked for.

Margot shook her head helplessly, trying to get herself under control. She longed to tell her mother all of it but was acutely conscious of their half-hour time limit and felt constrained by it. There was no way on earth she could air all her fears and experiences in so short a time. She also knew that once she started talking about all of it, she'd go on for hours, days. She wished she could simply stay with her parents, not to go back with Paul. But she couldn't. She knew if she made a move like that Paul would make all their lives so wretchedly miserable that she'd eventually return home with him in order to restore peace to her parents' lives. She could so clearly see Paul torturing all of them, threatening, making phone calls. All sorts of things.

She didn't feel she could inflict this on two other people, people she loved.

If you'd only take the first step, Ingrid thought. If you would only say what you feel, talk to me about what is happening. Then, there would be room to talk in, room to decide in. But you will not allow me in. No one can help you if your shame prevents you from asking for help. You cannot receive help until you are ready to admit you need it. Speak to me! Let us help you! We love you. We want to help.

Everything inside her was shouting at her to tell her mother. But she couldn't get her mouth to open and allow the words out. She was intimidated by the image of Paul playing hell with more lives. She drew away from her mother and fumbled in her handbag for some tissues.

"Do you remember George from the office?" Ingrid asked, watching Margot wipe her eyes and nose, thereby removing some of the makeup she'd used to camouflage her bruises.

Margot nodded.

"He has been a drunk for years. Oh, very quietly. A pleasant drunk. A man who begins drinking midmorning and drinks steadily until he goes to sleep at night. Everyone loves George. For years we had been trying to get him to admit he had a problem. George would smile and listen to all that was said, then go back to his desk, open the bottom drawer and take out his bottle to have another drink. Then, something happened. No one knows precisely what. But suddenly George was no longer drinking. His desk drawer was empty. He began to shed years, looking younger; to make decisions, producing his columns on time. And very good columns.

"Finally, the managing editor asked him directly. George told him he awakened one morning feeling sick, sick as on every other morning. But especially sick on this particular morning. And suddenly he hated what he was doing to himself. 'I'm a drunk,' he said to himself. 'I am a drunk and I need help.' He went to Alcoholics Anonymous and got help. What he said finally when the managing editor approached him was, 'I'm an alcoholic. I wasted almost twenty years of my life trying to pretend I wasn't.' Charles, the managing editor, said he had never loved George more than he did at that moment. Do you understand what it is I'm saying to you, Margot?"

Margot didn't answer. She couldn't.

"I am telling you that unless you admit you have a problem, you can do nothing to cure it." She paused, hoping Margot would say something, anything. "There are people who love you, Margot," she said softly, her voice threatening to give way to tears. "You are not alone in the world." She paused again, but still Margot didn't speak. "We must get some chives," Ingrid said at last. "I would not like to arrive back without them."

✠   ✠   ✠

After Margot and Paul had driven away, Ingrid sat down heavily on the sofa and rubbed her knuckles into her eyes.

"She will not talk about it," she said, laying her arms across her knees. "She will not talk and not talk, and he will beat her to death."

"I don't want him in my home," Jacques said, his eyes burning with indignation and anger. "I don't want him here!"

"You cannot do that to Margot," she said reasonably. "This is her home."

"There must be something we can do."

"Nothing. There is nothing. Sometimes, I ask myself if it is because of the way I am, the type of person that I am. I am not chatty or the light-hearted type of mother. And I wonder if it would be easier for her to talk to me if I was that sort of woman. But when I think about it, I know I am merely making excuses for Margot, not for myself. She *knows* we care, that we love her. But until she chooses to take the first steps, until she looks and sees and admits to herself what is happening, there is no help for her. She would not accept it from us because she is too proud to admit her mistakes. It would do no good forcing ourselves on her."

"I don't believe she loves him," Jacques said. "I don't believe it! No one could love that man. A man who beats his wife. It isn't love."

"She's not stupid," Ingrid said, trying to reason it through. "She's not in the least stupid. So why does she stay? Can you explain it to me? Can you tell me how someone like Margot, with her intelligence, can keep on with a man like that?"

"I don't understand it." Jacques sighed.

"I will tell you," Ingrid said angrily. "It is like George with the drinking. You can talk and talk and give advice to people like that. But unless they listen, unless they admit to the problem, all the words, the talking and advice mean *nothing*. She would agree and agree, then go back to him believing she can change him, that next time it will be different. It will *never* be different. She has not learned that you cannot change people."

"How can you know how it is?" He felt too old and tired to be facing his daughter's problems when she was unwilling to face them herself.

"It is so obvious! He has become a habit to her. She is making herself accept his brutality as her lifestyle. Telling herself he loves her, justifying his actions. There is no love there!" she exclaimed, feeling she would collapse under the weight of her impotency. "God! Why won't she *see?*" She lowered her head onto her arms and closed her eyes, praying for Margot to see.

"Weak people," he said, placing his hand upon her head. "They have such a way of robbing the strong of their strength. He will make her weak, make her sick as he eats her strength. I am so afraid for her. Even if she could not come to us, there should be some place where she could go, people who could help her."

"Nothing," she said, raising her head to meet his eyes. "It is the worst pain of my life to know there is nothing we can do and nowhere for her to go. Unless she comes and says, Help me! And I fear she will never come, never ask."

✠   ✠   ✠

It was her Mustang, not the Thunderbird that broke down. She was terrified that Paul would use this mechanical failure as an excuse for beating her again. But he looked at the repair estimate, balled it up in his hand and said, "Fuck it! Let's buy a new car and get rid of that wreck! In fact, let's get rid of both of them. I've had it with these wrecks! What d'ya say, Louis baby?"

Astonished, she said, "All right," not daring to question his decisions.

They went out that same evening to look at cars and Paul bought himself an MG and a small-sized Buick two-door sedan for her. Both old cars were accepted as trade-ins and Paul—to her further amazement—wrote out checks, paying cash for both cars.

"Made a little money on the market," he said casually, making no further reference to the amount he was spending for these two brand-new cars.

His MG would take three weeks to arrive. But there was a model on the lot available for her and the very next morning she was driving into town in her new car, trying to comprehend the devious turns of Paul's brain.

Wilma said, "Haven't seen you in a couple of weeks. I thought you might've gone off for a trip or something."

"I had the flu," Margot lied, standing at the counter with her purchases: an omelet pan—she'd never cooked an omelet in her life—and two orange and white gingham pot holders.

"I was thinking," Wilma said, ringing up the sale, then wrapping the pan in tissue. "A group of us play cards one afternoon a week. You might like to come."

"What sort of cards?"

"Poker? Do you play?" Wilma smiled.

"What afternoon?"

"Wednesday. Can you make it?"

"I'd love to."

Paul telephoned that evening to say he'd be spending the night in town. Business. Relieved, she covered the casserole she'd prepared in foil and put it in the freezer. She wished he'd spend every night in town. When he wasn't there in the evenings, she felt she could almost tolerate the house.

She made herself a cup of tea and a cheese sandwich and settled down in the living room to watch television. She was on the verge of slipping into consideration of her present circumstances and how and when she might change them when a program in progress on the Public Television Network drew her attention. A show on heart disease and what to do in the event of someone suffering a heart attack. Fascinated, she watched the demonstrations of heart massage and mouth-to-mouth resuscitation. She absorbed the details as the fireman on-screen demonstrated with a horribly lifelike dummy whose heart and throat were exposed to show the results of these life-saving efforts.

For some reason, she saw herself as the dummy; her throat exposed, her chest wall opened to reveal her lungs, her heart. If only, she thought, my life could be saved so simply.

When the show ended, she was disappointed and got ready for bed in a totally distracted state of mind, thinking over the routines the fireman had explained, macabrely wondering if, by reversing the process, you could kill someone with that technique. Placing your mouth over his, inhaling fifteen times instead of exhaling; placing all your weight over his heart stilling it; refusing to allow it to go on beating. I am going mad, she thought, getting into bed. I have to stop thinking this way.

✠   ✠   ✠

Wednesday afternoon, Margot pulled up in the driveway at Wilma's house—an old Colonial clapboard dwelling, with black shutters, a weathervane on the roof and a fieldstone front walk—anticipating a pleasurable afternoon, possibly losing a few dollars. But something to do, new people to meet.

Wilma, looking very pleased to see her, ushered her into the dining room where four other women—all looking and sounding deadly serious about the game they were starting—lifted their heads as Margot and Wilma came in.

"Meet the girls," Wilma said, introducing them.

Janet. About forty-five with a sharp, keen-eyed face and a hard handshake. Her rings cut into Margot's hand. She had short, bleached blonde hair and very expensive coordinated separates on a tiny, bony, breastless frame. Her smile flashed on for a count of three, then flashed off again and she returned to the cards she was shuffling with all the dexterity and panache of a Mississippi riverboat cardsharp.

Lucie. From Texas. She volunteered the information that her husband had just been transferred here from Chicago where they'd lived for the previous two years. Softly overweight with billowing breasts straining the front of her short-sleeved angora sweater; her thighs spreading danger-

ously against the seams of her double-knit trousers. Her
hand was soft and moist, limp. Her eyes were equally soft
and moist. Her smile tremulous, begging for approval.

Joy. From the city. About twenty-three or -four.
Brown-haired, brown-eyed, a cupid's bow mouth and a row
of brilliantly even white teeth. A splendidly proportioned
body with upthrusting breasts and trim, meatless hips. She
looked very young and terribly nervous, as if this was one
of her first forays in the world of adult women. Her hand,
though, was warm and dry, solid. She smiled eagerly,
searching Margot's eyes for several seconds before withdrawing her hand. The act of removing her hand seemed a
definitive one; as if Margot wasn't the one she'd been hoping to meet.

And Michelle. Fiftyish. With black, shaggy-cut hair,
exquisitely aristocratic features. A full, sensual mouth lip-
sticked in bright red. A long, beautifully formed nose and
large, haunted dark eyes. Giving the impression of tremendous sexuality with her rounded hips, slender legs—the
only one of the women present wearing a dress—sloping,
round breasts. Her wrists hidden beneath heavy gold
bracelets, her fingers weighted down with rings. She shook
hands, surprisingly, like a man. Firm, fast. But her tongue
slipped out to moisten her lower lip as she clasped Margot's
hand and peered intently into Margot's eyes.

Margot sat down, setting her purse on the floor beside
her. Wilma presented her with a glass of wine—they were
all drinking—then sat down too and the game began.

She'd been prepared for reasonable, even—in her estima-
tion—high stakes. But as five, ten and twenty dollar bets
were placed, she realized she was involved in genuine gam-
bling. Not a friendly, informal game, but one for high
stakes, with five people whose female attributes vanished,
leaving them as deadly serious, as bloodthirsty, as intent, as
paid assassins. She was in on every hand because of the

two-dollar ante, but folded as often as possible, even with good cards, when she heard the others begin raising their bets. Raising, ten, twenty. I'll see that and raise you ten. Margot placed her cards face down on the table, her under-arms running with perspiration as she watched the others fight their way down to the last call. They played through-out the afternoon, with only a short break of thirty minutes for food. Sandwiches from the kosher delicatessen in town. Tart pickles. Potato salad. Cole slaw. Lucie ate as if she was starving. Janet ignored the food as if it was contaminated. Joy ate the corned beef from her sandwich and left the bread on the plate. Michelle ate pickles and cole slaw, stat-ing. "I am on a diet eternally. Pickles have no calories, eh?" Wilma, looking amused throughout, ate even more than Lucie, downing two and half of the huge sandwiches, large quantities of the potato salad and cole slaw and a sizable slab of the chocolate cake she produced as dessert. Margot ate half a chopped liver sandwich wishing she could have been eating it anywhere else in the world because she'd never had a more delicious sandwich, but every bite was the consistency of sawdust in her mouth and nearly impos-sible to swallow.

Then the play recommenced. Margot made one attempt to excuse herself from the game but Wilma very pleasantly advised her, "We quit at four. You've got time to finish the game." And Margot pushed her ante into the pot. She won several hands but lost it all back in one reckless raising ses-sion and calculated she'd lost close to four hundred dollars by the time the game ended.

Janet was the big winner. Margot watched her counting her chips, guessing there had to be close to a thousand dol-lars there. Lucie was left-handedly writing out a check to Joy for three hundred and forty dollars. Joy looked not happy, not sad but simply, obviously relieved not to have lost. Michelle, apologetically, was signing traveler's checks over to Wilma. More than two thousand dollars had changed hands. Margot was panic-stricken. In paying out her losses, she used up almost all the money Paul had given her to deposit in the checking account.

Getting to her feet, she managed to smile and say good-bye to the other women and thank Wilma for inviting her. Then she fled out to the Buick and drove straight into town to the bank, praying she'd get there before the drive-in window closed. She transferred four hundred dol-lars from her personal savings account and deposited it in the checking account, then stared at her critically deplet-ed escape fund balance, feeling sick. Stupid. She'd been unbelievably stupid, naive. She'd gone ahead without ask-ing about the stakes and thrown away money she desper-ately needed if she was ever to get away from Paul.

And what kind of place was this, what kind of women? How could they afford to lose such large amounts of money? The more she learned of the town and its occu-pants, the more she felt as she had upon moving here: like someone who'd sneaked in under false pretenses.

✠　　✠　　✠　　✠　　✠

Nine

WHILE SHE WAS PREPARING PAUL'S DINNER—NAUSEATED by the sight and smell of the food—she thought again about that afternoon and about Wilma. She had, until today, thought of Wilma as someone uninvolved in the subterranean workings of the town; those workings Wilma spoke of frequently, scathingly, derisively. But Margot had to have been mistaken. Wilma might make remarks about her customers, might comment in crisp asides about the shoddy quality of life in this town and the pretentious, phony attitudes of the executive transients and their families who comprised the bulk of the town's population, but she was there right inside with them. Or else, cleverly taking advantage of these people. Was Wilma using them while pretending to be sympathetic? Was Wilma someone who talked a good show but who was up to her armpits in all those things she put down? If this was the case, she was definitely someone Margot would have to stay away from, someone unsafe to confide in. That was a pity because Margot had felt so attracted to her, had hoped Wilma might be someone who'd listen and understand Margot's problems, even possibly be able to help. That was out of the question now. She'd have to be very careful from now on, on her guard at all times with Wilma. She couldn't afford to risk any more losses.

What floored Margot was the fact that Wilma had revealed so much about the goings-on in town with such an air of disgust and sincerely affronted sensibility that Margot had assumed Wilma would assiduously avoid any direct contact, any personal contact with these bored, discontented women. Wilma was, Margot now decided, cultivating these people in order to survive financially in the town. This seemed to be the truth; especially when Margot recalled the look of superiority and above-it-all amusement that had clung to Wilma's face throughout the afternoon.

Divorced, childless, without alimony, Wilma was—she claimed—totally dependent on her income from the shop. She frankly admitted that the income was there to be made but the hours and effort involved in keeping the shop functioning successfully took their toll. Insomnia, Valium for her shot nerves, an inability to gain weight.

Margot had been building up a private cache of sympathies that now were dissolving, scattering. It was sad having it happen because Wilma was her only direct contact with this town. She'd needed Wilma, had seen her as a source of honest interest, a very human contact.

While she was still actively debating the pros and cons of Wilma, Wilma telephoned to say, "Wasn't that something? Thank God I'm a lucky player or I'd go broke."

Margot felt slightly reassured.

"You're not upset, are you, Margot?" Wilma asked, considerately.

"Oh, no. No."

"Good! If I hadn't thought you could handle it money-wise, I wouldn't have asked you along." She laughed. "But I thought you'd enjoy seeing. Aren't they fierce, though? Did you ever see anyone as tough as Janet? Poker's not a game to her, it's a way of life. Get in there and *win*, baby! Take them for everything they've got. Next week the game's at her place. Then you'll really see some first-class hustling!"

"I'm not going to be able to make it," Margot said, trying to sound truthful. "I'm having lunch next Wednesday in town. With my mother."

"Too bad. Next time. Listen, I've got to scram. I'll catch you the beginning of the week. Stop in, have coffee."

"I will."

Paul was home. She heard the car door slam and instantly tensed up, turning back to the stove to attend to his dinner.

"Where were you this afternoon?" he asked offhandedly, leaning on the counter, watching her, drinking his martini.

"I had lunch with Wilma and some friends of hers." She was hot, starting to perspire again.

"I tried to call you half a dozen times. I was beginning to think something had happened to you."

"Lunch," she said. "It started late, ended late. Do you mind if I don't eat with you? I'm still full from lunch."

"Sure," he said lightly. "Come keep me company while I eat."

She glanced up at him and managed to smile, wondering, Are you never going to talk about what happened? Or *did* it happen in your mind? Are you pretending it didn't?

He ate with his usual titanic appetite and she watched, trying to pay close attention to what he was saying. Her mind kept sneaking away back to the afternoon, and back before that, hearing Wilma as she'd leaned against the counter in Noah's Ark, saying, "You wouldn't *believe* these women! Their kids despise them. They despise their kids. They do nothing all day, then the minute their husbands come through the door at night they hit them with a bus-load of complaints and demands. They're bored stupid, haven't a clue what to do with themselves now that the kids are big enough to stay out of the house most of the time. The men are off to the city early, not home until six-thirty or seven. If they manage to get home at all. Half of them are busy knocking off their secretaries or nice little twenty-year-olds who don't give them any hassles, none of the grief. To those girls in town, they're Mister Terrific. It's heavy ego-fodder, lets them forget the pain-in-the-ass kids always whining about something and the wives who don't turn them on anymore because all they ever bring to bed with them is a list they've been preparing all day of all their grievances.

"Mr. Terrific isn't interested in hearing any of it, so out go the women, looking for something else. And if they can't find it ready-made, they create it. Politically, they're all way over on the right although they talk a terrific liberal line. And they're busy with great acts of good. Beautify Main Street. That's a biggie. Or the House Tour. Get your house on the tour. Or the garden group. Something."

"I've got to take the MG in for adjusting. It's idling too fast," Paul was saying when she tuned back in. "I'll need you to drop me at the station tomorrow and pick me up when I get back."

"Yes. Okay," she said, preoccupied. Something critical was happening not only to her life but to life all around her. She badly needed time to think it through.

Sexually, Paul was keeping his distance. And she was grateful. He hadn't touched her since the night of the beating. And every night when he climbed into bed beside her, she clenched her fists, ready for his advances; prepared to suffer them through. But he kissed her chastely on the forehead most nights and instantly fell asleep, while it took her close to an hour to come back down from her fearful preparedness. Slowly, slowly, she'd back away from her fear and her body would uncoil, finally allowing her to sleep. But her sleep was far from restful. She had dreams of bloodshed, mutilation, episodes of bestiality. She'd awaken two or three times a night in terror, her heart hammering, the hair at the back of her neck dripping with perspiration. Her mouth dry, her eyes wide, staring into the darkness, she'd turn to look at the mound of Paul's soundly sleeping body, then silently sink down again, to lie smoking a cigarette, waiting for her brain to change reels so she could go back to sleep.

Without consciously being aware of starting, she'd become a heavy smoker; had grown herself a habit, a dependency upon thirty or forty cigarettes a day. She seemed never without one. Her fingers closed around the thin stem of a cigarette, her lungs expelling clouds of acrid smoke—she was buying cartons of illusory comfort. And her weight was going down, down until her clothes fell over her body shapelessly. She derived a kind of grim, fatalistic satisfaction from the sight and feel of her shrinking body. Walking proof of the tortures inflicted upon her. Paul had to see and feel guilty, knowing she was dying because of him. He was killing her. If she grew gaunt enough, frail enough, he'd notice and make amends, lose the vacancy in his eyes, return to himself. Something had to happen.

The next morning, she took him to the station, noticing—hearing Wilma's voice like a narration—dozens of fake-wood paneled station wagons all driven by women, dropping off dapper-dressed men, all shaved, shorn and ready to face the day. While half-dressed or coat-over-nightgowned women—some with small children shrieking in the back seats—saw them off before backing out, driving away to face their senseless day.

That evening, when she arrived at the station, there were rows of double-parked cars without occupants. At most, there were three other cars she could see with anyone in them. She lit a cigarette and looked around, wondering where everybody was. The platform was deserted. She turned in her seat to look at the row of stores facing the station. Restaurant. Liquor store. Plant store with its window full of wilting greenery. Another restaurant. French. A tiny shop with tennis dresses displayed in the window. Her eyes traveled back to the first restaurant. The place was alive with people, half a dozen making their way in the front door; the upper half of the window (the lower half curtained-off) revealing a mass of bodies all pressed together in a dull orange light.

"Oh, that's Harry's Place," Wilma explained the next time Margot saw her at the shop. "If you want to know whether the trains are running on time, you call Harry's. You don't bother calling the station. Harry's has a tie-line to the city, so they know about the trains before the station does. How it works: Mrs. Such-and-So calls up and gets the word the five-forty's going to be late, then she hops into the car and heads for Harry's, all innocence, to wait out the extra hour. Doing her wifely duty, waiting to pick up Mister at the station. How was she to know the train was delayed? In the meantime, there's a whole trainload of happy fellows who came in on the three-forty but who told their wives they'd be on the five-forty. So, for a couple of hours, you've got a whole gang of mismatched Misters and Missuses all playing switchies. I wish I owned the damned place. I'd be rich."

Margot could scarcely believe it. There were more and more things going on in town she'd never noticed, hadn't heard about and wouldn't have known of. Except for Wilma. Wilma knew everything, apparently. And vocally condemned much of it. So, Margot wondered, why, if she found it all so repellent and shoddy, did she stay? She simply didn't know what to make of Wilma, stopped trying to determine Wilma's stance and stayed on to acquire more information. The more she heard, the more naive she felt. Paul had been right in many ways, about her years of academic life. She'd been sheltered at the university, protected from all sorts of realities. Now, through Wilma, she was getting an entirely new kind of education and, in the process, drawing daily closer to formulating conclusions based on what she saw and heard.

There was a parallel she was tracking here; one that seemed to be running just beyond the periphery of her life with Paul and she had a compulsion to continue finding out, positive her exposure to the shadowy underside of the town's life would clarify her own position.

Three weeks after the fact, having kept his distance for that time, Paul made his first sexual overture. She was almost asleep—having assumed he'd fallen with his usual alacrity into his peaceful little boy's sleep—when she felt his hand moving upward between her thighs. She had to tell herself not to resist. Relax. Relax. Don't fight him, let it happen.

To her surprise, she responded. And relaxed.

"Let me," he whispered, caught up in his own excitement. "Let me."

She scarcely heard him, hearing only the treacherous hum of her own body as it throbbed, vibrating beneath his hands, his mouth. He turned her onto her stomach and she went willingly; divorced, as always, from her body's practices.

"This way's better," he whispered, his fingers working over her, inside her, driving her deeper into need. "Hold still," he instructed.

Initially, she thought he was overeager, misdirected in his haste. But she quickly realized he intended this, wanted it—had done it before—and said, "No, Paul. Please. I can't!"

He was busy behind her and he had her held in such a way that it was impossible for her to turn, so she couldn't see what he was doing. The desire he'd created in her fled as he held her steady, then plunged ahead, making her scream as he gripped her hips, then frantically changed positions, lying over her back, his hands clutching her breasts as he compounded the pain, thrusting higher, harder; going on until she was weeping uncontrollably, her eyes locked shut against the rending pain.

He finished and his voice whispered into her ear, "Didn't I tell you it's better this way? Fantastic! Did you come?"

She couldn't bear it. Asking if she'd come, talking about how much better this was. He was living in another world, his brain shrouded in preferred interpretations; seeing what he wanted, hearing what he wanted. Selective reality. He was dragging her headlong into the depths of madness. And she could do nothing. If she spoke out—of pain, of displeasure, of shock—he'd beat her. And she couldn't physically withstand anything more. She'd arrived at the end of all her resources—physically, mentally, emotionally.

He withdrew and she gasped, clapping her hand over her mouth, praying, No more. Please, no more. Leave me alone now!

"I'm still turned on," he murmured, pressing his face into her belly. "Christ! Isn't that the best?"

He lifted her leg over his arm and pushed his mouth at her. She was empty, feeling nothing. Her body twitched every so often as he hit a particularly sensitive spot. But that was all. And she began to despair now of her visible lack of response. If she didn't come—perform to order— he'd become angry, perhaps hit her for not reacting. She could hear him shouting at her, What do you think I'm *doing* this for? And tried to sweep clear her brain, commanding her body to perform. Please God, let me come! Let me come so this can end! I'll never ask for anything else ever again. Just let me get past this. Let me come so he'll stop!

He was determined that she would and, finally, feeling oversensitized, abraded, the spasm took her. She collapsed in a wet heap and he got up, looking highly pleased, and

went into the bathroom. She lay without moving, overwhelmed by self-disgust, pain and residual contractions
that renewed the pain he'd bestowed upon her insides like
some sort of malicious gift.

When he emerged from the bathroom, freshly showered,
powdered and ready for sleep, she got up unsteadily and
walked slowly into the bathroom, not daring to let the
tears come until she was safely beneath the noisy refuge of
the shower.

Her heart skipped abnormally, her breathing was the
noisy rasp of someone who'd run a race. She felt dehuman-
ized, ruined. There was little remaining for him to do but
kill her. And that, she thought, was the next and final step.

This is better.

He'd been doing that with other women. Or other men.
And he'd formed a preference.

I've got to get out of here, get away. Mama's right. I've got
a problem. I can't be helped until I admit that. I admit it.
Oh God! It's true. I've got a problem. His name is Paul.
He's thirty-three years old. And he's sick.

✠   ✠   ✠   ✠   ✠

Ten

THE FOLLOWING MONDAY MORNING, WILMA TELE-
phoned.

"Listen, a group's getting together at my place Wednesday
afternoon. Why don't you come? You'll enjoy yourself,
have a good time."

"Cards again?"

"Not cards this week. Come about one. I've got to scram.
A new shipment just came in and there's nobody here to
help me unpack it. These damned girls get their periods
and go home for a week. See you Wednesday?"

"Yes, all right."

She'd have accepted almost any invitation if it meant
getting out of the house. Paul's things—his clothes, his tie
clips and cuff links, his cache of business papers, his mem-
orabilia—daunted her. She could scarcely bring herself to
touch his underwear, pushing it into the washing machine
with averted eyes as if by not seeing, she might not be
touching garments he'd worn next to his skin.

The house itself depressed and enervated her. The rooms
now seemed to be waiting menacingly. If she stepped into
one of the unoccupied bedrooms upstairs, she might van-
ish, never to be seen again. The expanse of hallway on the
second floor seemed to echo with ghostly whispers and she
wondered idly about ghosts, if the place possessed them. Or

would the ghosts come only after she and Paul left the house and some other couple or family took possession?

Having little else to focus on, her attention was split between speculations about Wilma and a replay of that half-hour spent with her mother in the car.

When she thought about her parents, part of her, childishly, wished that her mother and father had stepped in and interceded on her behalf—refusing to allow Paul to take her home with him. But the reasoning part of her knew she not only would never have allowed them to take such an action but also that she'd have been totally thrown by so direct a reversal of their roles. They'd always insisted it was her right to make decisions. But it was also up to her to suffer and enjoy the results of those decisions. And she knew that their refusal to interfere now came not because they didn't love her—their love being perhaps the only constant in her life she was sure of—but because they couldn't alter the patterns of a lifetime. They were not overly demonstrative, overly protective parents. And she'd always been glad of that. They were always available and had always been willing to sit down at the kitchen table and lengthily discuss the pros and cons of any given problem or situation. That was their way. She knew it and accepted it. All she had to do was pick up the telephone and call either one of them and there would follow a family discussion on what should be done. Just pick up the telephone, she told herself. But she couldn't. Not yet.

She wanted out, wanted to run as far from Paul as she could. Yet she seemed to lack the strength to make the initial moves. Constantly her brain still sought to excuse Paul's behavior. She seemed unable to break this habit of telling herself he was clever, gifted, possessed of too much energy, too much drive; all of which required an outlet. He was, she lied to herself, deeply grieved by his acts against her. He was this. He was that.

No, he's mad, she argued. I know now he is. I have to stop trying to justify his actions.

She no longer loved him. This knowledge made her feel so guilty, such a fraud she sometimes felt that leaving him would be the ultimate fraudulent act. She knew she shouldn't feel this way. But something inside her grieved over the loss of the love and still clung to the slender hope it could be resurrected. She battled this tendency toward wishful thinking with all the common sense she could muster. Common sense she believed she'd inherited from her mother. Remembering long, chatty strolls around Remington Park. As a child, she'd looked up and up into her mother's face, hypnotized by the sun-strewn nimbus of her mother's hair, and had known an inrushing of certainty and pleasure. Mama would always be there to explain things, her quiet voice naming the plants and shrubberies, detailing the growth process from seedling to full-grown plant. Mama was smarter, nicer, prettier than anyone else's mother. She talks to me, the child Margot had thought smugly, proudly. We have grown-up conversations and I'm not treated like I'm stupid just because I'm a little girl.

I loved her—loved them both—so much, felt so proud of them. The pride, the pleasure was like a big lump right in the middle of my chest and I carried it around inside me with a happy grin splitting my face, glad to carry the load of all that love with me. So glad there weren't any other children. Only me. So I didn't have to share them, didn't get the diluted dregs of their love but all of it. Everything. I depended on their willingness to communicate and married Paul believing I could transfer that dependency, that communicative lifestyle, to him. Without ever pausing to consider Paul's substance or whether he possessed the ability to communicate. I believed—if he didn't—that I could teach him how.

She turned to face her reflection in the bedroom mirror,

that other woman in the mirror. And saw that the eyes no longer slid away, reluctant to look, to see. The eyes met hers unflinchingly. They were filled with questions, with fear, with growing determination. I will not be defeated. I will not stay here. I will withdraw whatever money I have left and I will go. I will. Yes. I will.

But she'd have to wait for a propitious moment. She didn't want to leave a trail. She'd never return and didn't want to be found. She had no idea what she'd do or where she'd go. She only knew she was going to get out. And knowing—at least in her mind—that she was en route, she could tune Paul out, making appropriate responses to his questions and comments; holding herself still inside herself, insulated now by the knowledge that she'd finally managed to face the woman in the mirror and her two selves were becoming knitted into one.

Ceaselessly, she went backward over the mistakes she'd made, the masochism she'd displayed in the years of her marriage. All in a good cause, she'd told herself along the line. Because considerable effort was involved in making a marriage function successfully. But they hadn't ever had a marriage. It had been something else. She couldn't put a name to it.

Wednesday morning it was raining and cold. The false warmth of the early spring she'd been enjoying was gone. This sudden reversal in the climatic conditions seemed significant. After Paul had left to catch his train, having told her he'd probably have to spend the night in town, she walked through the house carrying her cup of coffee, trying to collect her determination. This was the perfect time to go. She'd have a full twenty-four hours—more—to put a great deal of distance between herself and her life until now.

Get going! Do it! Hurry!

Yes! She suddenly set her cup down and raced upstairs to

get dressed. She was running on instinct, having failed to establish any definite sort of plan. Dressed, she started to make the bed, then stopped. I don't have to do this. What I have to do is go to the bank and get my money. Yes, the money.

Hastily, she snatched up several articles of jewelry she wanted to keep. Then she stopped, deciding she'd come back to the house and pack a bag properly later. Be calm! she told herself. You've got all day, all night. Be methodical, orderly. Do this right!

She put on her raincoat, tied on a scarf, picked up her car keys and handbag and went out to her car. First things first. She'd go to the bank and withdraw her money. Then she'd have lunch in town. Or did Wilma say lunch? She couldn't remember. But she did want to see Wilma one last time, say good-bye without allowing it to be known it really would be good-bye. After all, regardless of Wilma's dubious stature in the town, she was almost the only friend Margot had made here.

She had to park several doors down from the bank and switched off the engine, preparing to get out of the car, when she noticed a Cadillac with the driver's door open, a woman sitting behind the wheel staring straight ahead of her.

Instantly, Margot felt something was wrong. Some mechanism in her brain alerted her to distress signals and she sat for a moment watching the woman in the car.

"She's ill." Margot put the signal into words in her mind as she got out of her car and moved quickly toward the sight of the blanched, elegant face and immobilized figure. She could see the fear in the woman's eyes. It showed in the way they focused; seemingly straight ahead but, in reality, inward; staring into the core of her interior, reflecting on the quality and intensity of her pain.

Margot knew that look. She'd seen it looking back at her

from her mirror in the house. Pain.

As Margot went closer, she became even more aware of the fine structure of the woman's face. She was perhaps fifty. Or younger. It was difficult to judge. She had a certain ageless quality.

"Are you all right?" Margot asked. The woman's eyes shifted and she turned slowly. She'd climbed out of the car as Margot had approached her. She was lovely, with delicate features. Margot wished, just for an instant, time would stop so she might properly absorb the loveliness of this face, the large blue eyes and high-boned cheeks, the full, soft-looking mouth and pointed chin.

She glanced at the car. It was, in its own way, equally beautiful: new, gleaming expensively in the freezing downpour, rejecting the flow of water with a waxed, almost human, disdain.

Looking back, the woman's eyes locked onto Margot's as they filled, moment by moment, with visible confusion and fear.

"Let me help you," Margot offered, extending her hand, her heartbeat quickening. "I'll help you."

The woman's fingers retained a resolute grip on the top of the car door as her eyes, now fully registering the impact of what was happening to her, darted from side to side before returning to Margot's face.

"I don't know what's wrong," she said almost inaudibly, the rain dashing unnoticed against her face. "I don't know."

Hearing the woman's voice did something strange inside Margot's head, creating in her the remarkable sensation that she was flying backward in time, that this was something that had happened before. And the words exchanged and the gestures had an aura of familiarity to them. Margot was gripped by the knowledge of impending loss, making her desirous of saying, all kinds of things—intimate, important things—to this woman she didn't know. "She's dying," she thought, her heart racing now as the older woman's face contorted suddenly and Margot realized why it all seemed so familiar. That television program she'd watched. This woman was having a heart attack.

"Please let me help you! I'll take you somewhere ... Out of the rain. I could call someone for you. Is there someone I could call? Let me help you, *Please!*" I'm begging, she thought, stunned. I'm begging her to let me make restitution. For what? My life for yours.

The woman swayed, then sank down onto the seat of the car, surprise making her eyes appear to glitter as they clung to Margot's.

"I'm sorry." She tried to smile as she examined Margot's face. "I've frightened you. I'm afraid I've frightened myself. It's nothing, I'm sure." But the smile vanished as her handbag fell to the ground and her hand became a fist pressing tight against her chest. "My God!" She exhaled, her nostrils pinched together, her body curving forward around her fist. "Oh, dear *God!*"

"I'll get someone," Margot said, unwilling to move, afraid to leave. "You need a doctor."

"Don't leave me!" she cried, grasping Margot's proffered hand. "I ..." She groaned, her eyes squeezing shut. Her hand was an iron clamp around Margot's. And then the hand, the entire left arm was shaken in a spasm as the woman fell sideways against the seat, her eyes rolling back in her head; her face turning dark red, almost purple.

Margot scooped up the fallen handbag, shoved it into the driver's well, then reached to touch the woman's throat. She couldn't feel anything. Four minutes. Four minutes to prevent brain damage. "No," she whispered, frantically opening her own bag, fumbling for the pocket mirror which was instantly rain-soaked and useless for the purpose she'd had in mind. She jammed it back into the bag which she flung aside as she bent over the woman. She managed to get the fur coat open and shoved her cold hands inside, searching for a route through the woman's clothing, finding it, feeling apologetic, whispering, "I'm sorry, I'm sorry," as she reached past buttons and silk and borders of lace to lay her hand under the woman's breast. Nothing. I'm sorry my hands are so cold, she silently told the woman, forcing her fingers down harder. There has to be something! she thought. There *has* to be. But the woman didn't move, wasn't breathing. Margot sobbed involuntarily as she withdrew her hands, feeling she'd somehow committed a profoundly sacrilegious act in touching this unconscious body. She pulled the woman's coat closed and glanced around in desperation, for the first time noticing the small knot of people standing on the sidewalk near the front of car, watching.

"Please!" she cried, wounded by their uncaring passivity. "Get an ambulance! Call the police!"

Only four minutes. And one of those gone. She maneuvered the woman down onto the seat, towing her completely inside out of the rain, pulling the car door closed before climbing over to the passenger's side, kneeling as she opened the woman's mouth, thinking, It can't be too late! and drew the air from the woman's lungs with her mouth, then inhaled and pushed air into the lifeless body, trying to concentrate on remembering the procedure she'd seen the fireman demonstrate.

She thought fleetingly of how it must look—kneeling with her mouth over this woman's, then placing her two hands beneath the exposed breast, exerting pressure. She looked at the woman's breast, a distant part of her mind recording, How young her body is. Not in the least old. No. She couldn't allow anything to make her deviate from the counting, the resuscitation. She thrust everything extraneous from her mind, concentrating on bearing down fifteen times, then the breathing; trying to make the lungs take in air, trying to force the heart to recommence its independent rhythm. Tear ran down her nose and dropped onto the woman's face and she silently said, I'm sorry, sorry, deploring treating her this way, revealing her narrow, youthful body to those heartless watchers in front of the car.

Please, she prayed, Breathe! *Breathe!*

Nothing. Another minute passed. She was losing time. Her hands were becoming cramped, her mouth stretched, her lungs aching. The only sounds she could hear were those she was making and that litany inside her head: Breathe! Breathe!

She kept on until she knew it was too late. She was kneeling, looking at a dead face, thinking, I lost you. How did I lose you? And why didn't they help? How could they just stand there and watch without helping?

Carefully, tenderly, a painful thudding in her own chest, she adjusted the woman's clothes, then drew the coat together. She closed the mouth and eyes and, trembling now, opened the passenger door and climbed out. She confronted the people on the sidewalk, shouting. "Get away from here! Go on! Get *away!*" Several of the people backed away, eyeing her as if she was completely crazy, but one man, in shirt sleeves, looking frozen, came forward.

"I called for an ambulance," he told her, putting his hand on her arm to steady her. "Is it your mother?"

She looked up into a middle-aged face of great kindness and eyes so dark they seemed bottomless. Feeling that kindness blanketing her, she fell into the protection of the man's arm, crying, "I didn't even know her. She's dead."

She wept, overwhelmed by grief. She had an aching desire to climb back into the car and gather the woman into her arms and hold her; fashion some loving act with which to say good-bye, to atone for the indignity of dying this way. Alone. While a crowd of curious passersby stood and watched. What kind of place was this where life seemed of so little value or importance?

"Come into the shop," the man was saying, drawing her in out of the rain. A book store. She stood shivering just inside the doorway, watching—feeling totally separated, outside this scene—as the man poured coffee into a paper cup and pressed it into her hand.

"You appeared to know what you were doing," he said, urging her to drink the coffee.

"How could they just stand there and *watch?*" she asked him, her hands being thawed by the heat of the coffee. "How could they just *watch?*"

He shook his head sadly, pulling on an old cardigan.

"It's safer, just watching," he said softly.

They were standing, looking into each other's eyes as a patrol car screamed up, followed by an ambulance. And it became then a matter of imparting information, giving details, surrendering personal relevances as to who she was and where she lived and how she'd come to be the only actual witness to this death. She couldn't bear it, couldn't abide describing how she'd been about to go into the bank when she'd noticed the woman in the car.

She wanted instead to consider all the thoughts that had occurred to her while helplessly attempting to save that life; to get away somewhere to think about this death. Because it directly related to her in a highly significant way she had to analyze. It had to do with her life.

Who was she? she wondered of the woman. Who'd loved her? She'd been loved, Margot could tell. She'd had that look, that relying vulnerability of someone accustomed to allowing herself to be protected. She shivered, thinking of placing her cold hands on that still-warm, scented flesh; thinking of the fantastic fragility of life—so illusory, so suddenly lost. My life, she thought, is being lost. Hourly, daily.

The police said she was free to go and she turned and ran

out of the shop, back to her car, forgetting where it was she'd been going only a short time before. She forgot everything but the fiercely urgent need to go somewhere and examine what had happened and how it affected her. Because—God!—it affected her.

Still crying, she drove from the shopping center, heading back to the house, then pulled over to the side of the road. She didn't want to go back to the house. She leaned against the car door and closed her eyes, shivering, then opened them to look down at her dripping coat, then at her watch. After twelve.

Who had died, after all? For a moment, she wasn't sure if it was herself who had or a woman whose name she didn't know. A woman who'd had a girl's body, a young girl's firm, tender breasts and smooth, well-cared-for skin. It was that body, that touch of her skin that had to be, at least in part, responsible for this strange schism in her brain. She couldn't relate the flesh she'd touched—the body—to the head it had borne. That face. Tiny, multiple lines around the eyes; curved tracings parenthesizing the sensual mouth. The face came into sharp definition in front of her and she was bent with grief. I can't die, she thought. I haven't had a life.

She saw herself back there in the parking lot, her hands delving past the fabric surfaces to lay themselves on that silken skin; her mouth covering that other mouth, insisting the woman accept the life she was trying to give. A dead woman lying on the front seat of a Cadillac. I loved a dead woman. I loved you. You were alive and I loved you. You're dead and now I've got to save another life: mine.

They had stood there, sheltered by the bank awning and watched, spellbound. They *watched*. Paul could beat me to death right there in that same parking lot and these people, these residents of this expensive town, would stand by and watch him do it. I'm not safe here. Because this is a place where someone can die and people will stand at a safe distance and watch. It's not just Paul. It's this place, these people. All of it.

She'd go to Wilma's, stay an hour. No more than an hour. Then she'd go to the bank and get the money. First Wilma's. Then the bank. Perhaps Wilma would understand about the woman in the car, about what had happened. And at that moment, Margot didn't want to be alone. The possibility that Wilma might lend a sympathetic ear drew Margot toward her.

Wilma came to the door in a robe, smiling

"I'm a little early," Margot said quickly. "Something happened ..."

"Come on in," Wilma said, swinging open the door. "You're not too early."

Margot stepped inside, her eyes noting the darkness of the house; wondering why all the curtains were drawn. She turned, watching Wilma close and lock the door, anxious to tell Wilma about the woman in the car.

"In here," Wilma said, draping her arm across Margot's shoulders, ushering her into the living room.

Initially she couldn't believe what she was seeing. It had to be some sort of crazy trick her eyes were playing on her. Something delusionary. Her brain was still in a state of shock. But no. As she became accustomed to the dim light, she saw faces she recognized. Her bank manager. The man who owned the exclusive imported shoe salon on Main Street. The proprietor of the charming Italian restaurant she and Paul frequented. Several other men. And the women who'd played poker. Michelle, the Parisian who'd apologized over her traveler's checks. Lucie, the softly spreading Texan. Young Joy. Janet, the grim gambler. Two or three others. All naked. All engaged with the men or with other women. A frieze. The air reeking of perfumed perspiration; the salty smell of aroused flesh, spilled semen.

She stood staring into the room, aware that Wilma was dropping her robe, and she turned to see Wilma climbing onto the lap of the bank manager, straddling his lap, dipping her full-breasted body into his greedy hands.

Margot took a step backward, still gaping wide-eyed at the people assembled in the room; hearing—as if from a great distance—Wilma's voice beckoning her to, "Come on in. Come on." And her own interior voice saying, "This isn't happening! I don't believe it! Not when people are outside dying. This entire town. They're all mad. All of them. Except for that kind, tired man in the bookstore. One human being. Just one. I've got to get out of here. Out!"

She turned and ran.

Blanking her mind to the image of Wilma in the bank manager's lap, she drove directly back to the bank to withdraw the balance of her savings account. She stood, her foot tapping, her fingers drumming on the counter, the air rattling in her lungs, breathing fast while the teller counted out the bills. She grabbed the money and flew out. To the bookstore. Where she opened the door and looked in to see that the proprietor—that dark-eyed, gentle man—was busy with a customer. And there was no time to wait, to try to explain to him that he was the only one, finally, she wanted to say good-bye to. She closed the door and returned to the car.

Halfway to the city, she pulled into a service station and telephoned her mother.

"I have to see you. I'll pick you up in front of the paper in an hour."

"Are you all right?" Ingrid asked, alarmed by the tone of Margot's voice.

"I'm on my way now. I have to see you, talk to you. An hour."

Margot slammed down the phone and darted back to the

car.

The rain had stopped and, like some sort of miracle, the sun came out. Driving along the Old Shore Expressway, the glint of the sun on the water twinkling at the edge of her vision, she reviewed her circumstances; tried to calm herself sufficiently to think logically. Her dress, under the raincoat, was soaked with nervous perspiration. She was chain-smoking, the car filled with a thick gray cloud. An image of Paul arriving back at that empty house and his ensuing rage kept her foot pressed down on the accelerator. She drove on, moved by the fear that madness was contagious. I won't let that happen to me. I won't become like those women. I'm getting out, away. Going.

I have less than eight hundred dollars. I would have had more. But that poker game. Too many expensive games I've played in the last six years. All of them so costly. Yet I kept on, picking up the cards that were dealt to me; placing bets, wagering I could win. When the prize was nothing. Nothing. Merely the illusion of winning. Winning so I might die unattended in a parking lot. Afternoon sex with the men available, the ones who don't commute. While the husbands who commute are having afternoon sex with women in the city. Love. What's happened to love? I could never do that. Take off my clothes and climb into the lap of my bank manager. Wilma. She'd opened her thighs and slid herself over his body like someone trying on some article of clothing. For size. God! The bank manager. I couldn't. Afterward, every trip to the bank an embarrassment. The conversations revolving around, Will you be there next Wednesday? I didn't get to fuck you. I really wanted to fuck you but I had to take care of Wilma and then Lucie. And you know how Janet is. She has to win at everything. A hard case, has to be the one to get through all the men in the place. But I wanted you. You're not like the others.

That's right, I'm not. I won't donate my life to the town dump. I won't. I can't. I won't give up my brain, my rights.

She blinked, taking herself back to Remington Park, holding her mother's hand—strong, strong, mama's hand—gazing up into her face and the sky, all one; an infusion of love flowing from hand to hand. Giving that strength. It wasn't all for no good reason. I'm saving the only life I can—mine.

I have choices. I thought Paul was my choice. But I knew. I woke up on the morning after our marriage and looked at him, looked at the ceiling as if I thought I might see God there and I thought, What have I done? I've done something permanent here. And mistakes aren't allowed. It was too late. But nothing in my life is irremediable. How could I have believed as I did? Feeling I'd made the commitment, was obliged to see it through to the end of my days. Thinking, this is the way it is; thinking I was choosing someone to love when love had no place in that enterprise and my selectivity was nonexistent. My needs led me to the point of crucifying myself. I was nearly impaled through my palms on a cross of foolish pride and an encompassing desire to justify my decisions. Now I've been stopped in my tracks by a woman I loved more in my lack of knowing than I ever loved Paul with all my attempts at knowing. I have the capacity now to save only the life I have, and no capacity for standing by and watching as others around me dip and dance and die, all the while pretending it's life on an elevated plane. Death. My God! I've escaped.

Her mother was waiting. Margot pulled up. Ingrid opened the door and slid in.

"Are you all right?" her mother asked, her face pale with concern.

"I'm going. I wanted to see you first."

Margot found a place to park and turned off the car, then

shifted to look at her mother.

"I feel as if I don't have a lot of time," Margot said, urgency thrumming along her veins. "I feel as if I'm really running. I guess I am."

Ingrid's eyes filled and spilled over. She let out her breath, relieved. "Thank God!" she said. "I thought perhaps we were wrong, that there were things we should do. But I couldn't."

"You're glad!" Margot realized, feeling herself relaxing. "Oh my God!" she exclaimed, "Mama, so am I!"

They fell into each other's arms and Margot held on, conscious of her mother's scent, the strength of her body, its softness. She hadn't been wrong about that. The memory was a reality, was truth.

"Where will you go?" Ingrid asked. At that moment there seemed no difference between them. They were one, of an age. Contemporaries.

"Just away," Margot said, keeping hold of her mother's hands. "As far away as I can get. You weren't wrong. If you'd treated what was happening, if you'd treated me any differently, I'd have stayed to keep on proving you were wrong. Crazy, I know. But I would have. That story about George. Was it true?"

Ingrid nodded. "True. It was all true."

"I believed it."

"I hoped you would."

"Mama, I looked in the mirror and couldn't find me there. I couldn't see *me*. I could only see what I was becoming."

"Have you any money?"

"Some. Enough."

"Here," Ingrid said, opening her bag, removing her wallet. "Take this. I just cashed my check. Take it!"

Margot took the money.

"We couldn't interfere," Ingrid said softly, still feeling her ingrained habits of viewing everything—even her child—

objectively were responsible indirectly for Margot's having taken so long to admit the truth.

"You did the right thing," Margot said again. "I've always counted on you to be the way you are."

They embraced again, then Ingrid opened the door.

"One thing," she said as she was getting out of the car.

"Yes?"

"Remember this, Margot. All men are not Paul. Remember that," she said, stressing each word carefully. "I love you."

"Kiss papa for me. I'll write when I find a place where I want to stay."

Eleven

SHE DROVE ALL THAT AFTERNOON AND NIGHT AND stopped the next morning at a motel. She spent a sleepless, terror-ridden day and night in the motel tossing about on her rented bed haunted by visions of Paul finding her and slowly murdering her for her treachery. The next morning, she got up and went out to the car, driving on. She stopped for food, wanted to eat, craved food, but opened her mouth to the first bite only to find herself completely without appetite. She saw Paul's face and shrank inside, remembering how he'd beaten her, then raped her and calmly, afterward, eaten the dinner she'd been preparing.

She told herself not to think about him and bought several chocolate bars which she ate automatically as she drove, stopping frequently at highway service centers to buy cups of coffee, tea and soup. Feeling a kind of terrorized strength tightening the tendons in her arms and legs, forcing her forward; keeping her going. Until she was so dizzy, so exhausted her eyes started wandering from the road and she pulled off into a rest area on the side of the highway and sat for a long time before deciding she'd have to get off the highway and check into another motel.

She fell asleep instantly and awakened slowly, having difficulty breathing. And a pulsing pain in her lower abdomen. I've got a cold. From standing in that parking lot in the rain. She got up, thinking she'd go out and find a drug store, buy some aspirin, some antihistamine to help her breathe. But by the time she'd managed to dress herself, she knew something more serious than a cold was happening. She was shivering, yet sweating profusely; her hands shaking, her teeth chattering and the pain was gnawing at her lower belly, eating its way down into her thighs.

Scared, she followed the highway signs pointing the way to the nearest hospital and reeled in through the emergency-room doors to the desk where the nurse asked question after question and insisted on knowing how any treatment Margot might receive would be paid.

"Cash," Margot said faintly, holding on to the counter for support. "I'll pay in cash."

"Name of next of kin?"

She managed to give her parents' names and address before her hold on the counter dissolved. Her hands turned to water, her body became a stack of toppling sandbags and the walls and ceiling turned, turned as running footsteps thundered in her ears and she closed herself away from them, curling into a knot, a comma on the cold floor. Too late. She was dying after all.

✠ ✠ ✠

People seemed constantly to be trying to interrupt her sleep. They kept coming around whispering, touching and, angrily, she'd climb halfway out of sleep to tell them to go away, leave her alone. But they refused to stay away and finally she was forced to open her eyes and see that she hadn't died after all. There was a nurse with a tray on one side of the bed and a white-coated doctor on her right peering anxiously down at her. She stared at him, trying to make sense of all this; at the same time becoming aware of a new, different kind of pain in her belly.

"You're in intensive care," the doctor explained, his voice light and youthful. She looked at him more closely. She couldn't be sure this was real.

"We're moving you out of here," he went on, his soft light voice holding her captive as he explained that they'd been treating her for pneumonia and had had to get that under control before they dared administer anesthetic. For the surgery. To remove an ovarian cyst the size of a grapefruit. Non-malignant, fortunately. But of extraordinary size, requiring immediate removal. "Another week in bed and you'll be able to go home," he concluded, then stood waiting for her to respond.

"I'm all right, though?" she asked. "I can still have ... I mean ..."

"Oh sure!" he said confidently. "No problems. You'll be fine. It came out clean. You'll be a little sore for awhile but otherwise fine. Fine."

For a week, she was given medication, taken on slow tours of the corridors, and fed trays of soups, gelatins and cups of weak tea. Amazingly, she derived strength from this liquid diet. So that a week later she was at the main desk, handing over eleven of her thirteen hundred dollars, and dropping into a state of chaotic panic as she retrieved her car from the parking lot and headed back to the highway.

Two hundred dollars. She couldn't drive for very long; she was stiff weak, and she checked into yet another motel to take stock.

With thirteen hundred dollars she might have spent two or three weeks on the road, taking all the time necessary to decide on a future course; but with only two hundred dollars, she'd have to make some decisions at once.

She required a place to live, a job of some sort. Having listened to those executive wives complain about the problem of obtaining and keeping efficient, intelligent house-

hold help, it occurred to her that she might offer her serv-
ices as a domestic. It was one way that she might satisfy all
of her immediate needs with a single effort.

When she reached the next major city, she went to a
domestic employment agency whose ad in the yellow pages
seemed the most discreet and tasteful. The woman who
interviewed her responded with an eagerness and enthusiasm that led Margot to believe she'd instinctively made a
wise decision.

"We have so many positions," the woman said with a sin-
cere-looking smile. "Any of them would love to get their
hands on someone like you. You're free to relocate?"

"Absolutely free," Margot said, savoring the shape and
sound of those words.

"Marvelous! Let's start sending you out on interviews."

Four days of interviews. All of them with women who, in
one way or another, reminded her of the women in the
town she'd run from. Her money was almost gone. Mrs.
Burns at the agency said, "I've one position here I didn't
think would interest you. But maybe it would after all.
You're right to be choosy," she said encouragingly. "It's not
all that easy living cheek-by-jowl with people. How does
this sound: An elderly, bed-ridden man and his son. They
need someone to run their house, to cook, clean, shop for
groceries. Generally take care of everything. They're offering a private suite. Bedroom, sitting room, bath. Four hundred and fifty dollars a month. That's low for the job but
they might be willing to negotiate for the right person.
Would you like me to call, set up an interview?"

Margot agreed. She'd have to take this job because she
hadn't enough money to pay for another night in the
motel. Nervously, she listened as Mrs. Burns set up an
appointment, then to the directions Mrs. Burns gave her.

She set off, getting lost twice before finding the place. It
was a good distance outside the city, on a private road. A

huge house and very old, with gables and dormers, and surrounded by shade trees. This place looks haunted, she
thought, pulling up in front, leaving the car parked on the
circular driveway, but in good condition. The exterior was
newly painted pale gray with white trim.

The man who came to the door was tall and largely built
with a face that somehow looked wrongly put together:
shaggy black eyebrows that would have lent a brooding
appearance to his face except that his eyes seemed deep,
openly interested, and lit with humor; a long misshapen
nose that had obviously been broken at least once; a surprisingly well-shaped mouth that slipped upward into a
smile that made him younger-looking altogether, less forbidding; a heavy jaw, prominent chin; his skin very white,
his hair very black. The contrast was startling, like looking
at a black-and-white photograph that was supposed to
have been in full color.

His hand was warm, strong yet gentle, and he invited her
inside saying, "I was expecting someone a little older."

"I'm thirty-seven," she lied easily, adding ten years to her
age. At that moment she felt considerably older even than
that.

His eyes widened slightly so that he seemed amused as he
introduced himself. "I'm Cameron Harley," he said, leading
her into an obviously unused living room where dust hung
in the sunlit air. "Your name is Seaton, is that right?"

"Margot Seaton," she confirmed, looking at the oversized,
overstuffed, neglected furniture.

"Mrs. Perry left several weeks ago," he explained. "My
father's what you might loosely call 'difficult,' Mrs.
Seaton."

"Miss."

"Miss Seaton. Sit down, do." He perched on the edge of
a huge armchair, leaning toward her. "My father, as I started to say, can be difficult. To be truthful, we've had a lot of

problems with staff. He's not strictly bed-ridden. He simply prefers to stay in bed and issue orders from there. I'll tell you candidly this isn't an easy or rewarding job. Especially for someone as young as you—look." He paused, then reached into the pocket of his jacket for a pack of cigarettes and offered them to her. "Smoke?"

She wondered if it was some sort of trick question. Do you smoke? Yes I do. Sorry, we can't have someone around here who smokes. In none of her previous interviews—with women—had she been as bothered as she was now by every word and gesture of this man. And realized she was reacting with apprehension because he was a man. This is wrong, she told herself, saying, "Thank you," as she took one of his cigarettes and bent toward the match he extended. Her instincts made her want to get up and leave right then but practical considerations told her she was going to have to take this job—if only for a few weeks—because she'd used up her present alternatives. Eleven days in the hospital had taken most of her money. She had less than twenty dollars in her bag and no room booked for that night. So, no matter how she felt or what her instincts dictated, her decision was already made, had been when she agreed initially to the interview.

They both took deep drags on their cigarettes, using the time to study each other.

"What's wrong with your father?" she asked, anxious to hear him speak again. She did like the sound of his voice: deep, resonant, and humorous like his eyes.

"He had a massive coronary two years ago. He's recovered, but he likes to threaten people when they 'act up'— meaning not performing to his specifications—by feigning the start of another seizure." He laughed softly. "It can scare the living hell out of you the first time or two. After that, it's a little like a comic opera. There's not a thing wrong with my father. He just likes to see people hop."

"I see."

"To be a hundred percent honest, I'm getting a little desperate. I can't handle the house and my father's whims. I do a fair bit of cooking. Of necessity. But as you can obviously see, the place is getting away from me. Nothing a good vacuuming wouldn't remedy, I guess. I just don't have the time, though. I've managed to get in to my office once in the last three weeks. Not one damned thing would happen if he were left to his own devices here for one day but he has a gift for inflicting guilt and I'd just as soon do without the grief." He smiled again, apologetically.

"I understand," she said, sensing that this man had a great affection for his father.

"Mrs. Burns at the agency did say we're a little on the low side salary-wise. Depending on the person, we'd be willing to consider increasing it."

"You want someone to keep this place clean, cook the meals and argue with your father. Is that right?" She didn't want this job. A hell of a lot more than just vacuuming was needed. A hands-and-knees deep cleaning job. Even the baseboards were furred with dust.

Cameron was smiling again. "If he knows someone's intimidated by him, Dad'll jump in and bark away until he's reduced her to hysterics. Are you the hysterical sort, Miss Seaton?"

"I don't know. Maybe I am. I guess I won't know until I've met your father." Cameron was good-natured and witty, and she was terribly suspicious of these qualities.

"Well," he said, tipping his ash into a brass ashtray, "if you're up to it, why don't we find out right now? If you're not frightened off, we can get down to the logistics and start haggling over details."

"You mentioned your office," she said. "May I ask what business you're in?"

"I'm an importer."

"Of what?"

"Beans."

"Beans?"

"Beans," he repeated, smiling again.

"Oh," she nodded. "I see." She wanted to laugh, found his remarks and the situation very funny, but held herself in check.

"You're supposed to ask what kind." He laughed—a low rumbling sound. "You know. Baked. Jumping. Soy. Lima."

She did begin to laugh and stopped herself. He was delighted by her response and disappointed when she aborted the laughter.

"We might as well go on up," he said, getting to his feet, extinguishing his cigarette before once more meeting her eyes.

As they went up the stairs she couldn't help thinking what a splendid house it would be with new furniture and rugs, some wallpaper and bright paint. As it was, the faded, worn carpeting and old-fashioned, outdated furniture contributed to the dingy, depressing atmosphere.

He knocked at a bedroom door, opened it, then stepped inside and beckoned Margot to follow.

Seated in the center of a double bed against at least six pillows and looking surprisingly natty in blue and white striped pajamas sat Mr. Harley Senior, with white hair, a rosy, clean-shaven face and round blue eyes electric with intelligence.

"What in hell's *this?*" he demanded of Cameron. "Your latest girlfriend?"

"This is Miss Seaton," Cameron said calmly, that amused expression riding his eyebrows. "She's come to replace Mrs. Perry."

"A schoolgirl!" Harley Senior accused, directing his eyes to Margot. "What're you doing bringing schoolgirls into the house? You trying to put something over on me, Cam?"

"I am not a schoolgirl," Margot said quietly, thinking, this is a game he plays. He's not at all frightening. He's just— the idea touched a vulnerable spot inside her—a lonely old man. "I'm old enough to cook and clean a house," she said. She felt both physically weak and emotionally charged. The idea that she had nothing to lose hummed an underscoring countertheme in her brain.

"A big mouth!" Harley Senior's eyes grew calculating. "How come you're not home with kids instead of out looking for work?"

"If I had children, obviously I wouldn't be standing here bickering with you." Her cheeks were enflamed with color. She was being bold, rude, but it seemed called for. She was actually enjoying watching the changes play across the old man's face. He guffawed and threw out his hand in her direction.

"I like this one, Cam," he declared. "C'mere and shake my hand. Let's have a better look at you."

She advanced closer to the bed and placed her hand in his, smiling. She was riding along on instinct and her fear of the son and her instant affection for the father. There was something about this old man she recognized and intuitively understood.

"You're the skinniest damned bird I've about ever seen," he said, keeping hold of her hand, his eyes laughing at her now. "Probably can't cook worth spit."

"Just because I'm skinny doesn't mean I can't cook. I can probably cook better than anybody you've had around here."

Harley Senior's eyes flickered over at Cameron then back to her.

"You're not so tough," she said in a whisper, deriving an uncanny amount of pleasure from his very smooth hand still wrapped around hers. "Not so sick, either," she added, in an even lower whisper. "I think you're faking."

He leaned very close to her to whisper, "So're you, skinny."

Cameron watched the two of them, entranced. He'd never seen his father drop his guard so immediately. And he also wouldn't have believed this woman could be so easily prompted into gaiety. The two of them were definitely having a gay time baiting each other.

"I'll take you up on that bet," Harley Senior said loudly, releasing her hand. "Feisty. I like a feisty woman. Makes for good arguments. I like a good argument, too. Gets the blood circulating, shakes the dust outta the air. Like to argue?"

"In general. Not personal arguments," she answered.

"An academic type, eh?" he said sarcastically. "Got a whole string of little letters after your name, I'll bet."

"That's right," she said. "I do."

"Sonofabitch, Cameron! I *want* this one!" To Margot, he said, "You go on downstairs and fight some now with Cam about the details. When're you going to start all this cooking you like to brag about?"

"Now, I suppose."

"Go on, then. Go on! And don't you come up here to bring me any watery goddamned soup and cold toast!"

"You'll have to dress and come down for meals," she said, the boldness and a conviction of rightness taking firm hold of her. "I don't do room service."

The old man stared at her, open-mouthed. Cameron laughed out loud and opened the door. Margot looked over at him, then back at Harley Senior who waved his hand at her, saying, "I never yet met a skinny woman didn't think she was the cat's meow. Go on! But this better be one goddamned great meal!"

As they were going down the stairs, Cameron said, "I'll give you five hundred a month. If you stay, we'll talk about more later on. Would you like to see your rooms and the kitchen?"

"I suppose I'd better. Was I too rude? He seemed to expect a fight."

"Not at all. Dad expects *everything*. He rarely gets what he expects, though. I think you're going to be just what he needs. Mrs. Perry could handle the house well enough but Dad just defeated her. She spent an awful lot of time taking umbrage at everything he said." As he pushed open the swing door to the kitchen, he stole another look at her. You, he thought, are going to make an awful lot of changes around here. And I can't help feeling Dad's going to like it. So will I.

The kitchen was fairly modern with a dishwasher, a good stove, a freezer and refrigerator side by side, and miles of counter space. But horribly neglected, grimed with cooking spatters and grease.

"I'm a sloppy cook," he said, witnessing her slight grimace. "How about some coffee?"

"Thank you."

He occupied himself filling a percolator, then plugged it in and turned to her.

"I could bring your luggage in for you, if you like."

She hadn't any. Only a shopping bag filled with soiled clothes. She'd been buying bits and pieces along the way. But all her possessions, her clothes were back in the house with Paul. Except for half a dozen pieces of jewelry she'd dropped into her bag on the morning she left.

"What's wrong?" he asked.

"I haven't any luggage."

"None?"

"A shopping bag," she said.

"A shopping bag." He looked squarely into her eyes.

"I've been on the road. My luggage was stolen," she lied, forcing herself not to look away. "I haven't had a chance to replace what was taken." She felt suddenly tired, experiencing a twinge of pain.

"Well," he said, "we might as well have a look at your rooms while the coffee's brewing."

"All right," she agreed, grateful he wasn't going to pursue the matter.

My rooms. A suite. She stared into the sitting room furnished in mismatched castoffs. The bedroom was like a cell with a saggy-looking single bed that had neither head nor footboard, an ancient upright bureau topped by a lamp with a stained shade. She couldn't contain her sudden anger, her terrible disappointment.

"It's so ... neglected," she said, looking at him. Was he crazy, expecting someone to live here?

He saw how upset she was and turned to look at the room, then at her once more. "I'll concede," he said slowly, "this is pretty bad. But it's done for the others."

The implication was there: You're here as a housekeeper, not a guest. If you don't like what I'm offering, you don't have to stay.

"How many housekeepers have you had?" she asked.

"Quite a number," he admitted.

"Could I ask for just one thing?"

"What's that?"

"If you decide you're satisfied with my work, would you please replace that mattress? I'll pay for it myself out of my salary if you like. But the idea of sleeping in a bed ... all those other women ..."

She had managed to convey to him a dreary picture of an endless series of women all getting up, pushing back the blankets and then feeling about the floor for their slippers. Recalling some of the women who'd lived in this room, the image was anything but pretty. He nodded. "I think we can handle that. Why don't we go down? The coffee's probably ready by now."

"Mr. Harley?"

"Cameron. Call me Cameron."

"He really *is* all right, physically, your father? I mean, it wasn't wrong of me to say what I did about coming down for meals?"

He smiled. He seemed to face everything with a smile. "It was about the rightest thing anybody's done around here in ages," he said. "He needs a little shot every so often. I guess," he added, "we all do. Every so often."

Twelve

SHE FELT TOO TIRED TO DO ANYTHING BUT DUG IN AND superficially cleaned the kitchen, before scrambling together her first meal. There were few ingredients to work with but she managed to produce a meatloaf in mushroom sauce, scalloped potatoes and a salad.

"I'll be able to fix something a little more imaginative," she said, "when I've had a chance to shop for some groceries."

Cameron and his father ate everything she offered, complimenting her in their fashion.

Harley Senior said, "Not bad. Can't say I much care for your salad dressing."

Cameron said, "Delicious. Ignore him. He's convinced that if one complimentary word were to slip past his lips he'd be struck down on the spot by a bolt of lightning."

"You talk too goddamn much!" Harley Senior accused his son. "Where's the dessert anyhow?"

She cleared the dishes and produced the dessert.

Ice cream. "There wasn't anything else," she explained.

There was no response beyond a smile from Cameron, and she slipped back to the kitchen to lean against the counter and drink a cup of coffee while she tried to decide which job she'd tackle first in the morning. It was all so bad, so in need of attention that it was difficult to know where to begin. A huge hamper of laundry was waiting to be done. The washer and dryer, she'd discovered, were right there in the kitchen hidden behind louvered, folding doors. She'd get the washing started, then begin work on the kitchen. Once that was done, she'd go to the front of the house and do one room at a time.

"We'd like you to eat with us," Cameron said, coming through the swing door carrying the dessert dishes. "If that's all right with you."

"Yes, all right," she said, setting down her cup, wondering if that was customary. "I wasn't very hungry tonight. Are you ready for coffee?"

"Dad'll take his upstairs. I'll just pour myself a cup. I've got some work to do so if there's anything you need, I'll be in my office."

His office. "Where is that?" she asked.

"Third floor. Directly above your rooms."

"Okay."

She had to make up the bed. Under the ratty, damp-feeling chenille spread was an ominously stained mattress. She turned the mattress over only to discover an even uglier series of stains on the underside. She reversed the mattress once more and went out to find a worn-thin mattress pad in the linen closet and some clean sheets and blankets to make the bed. The idea of those stains made her feel sick. Someone had bled and/or wet in this bed, and she had to sleep on it. But she was bone-weary and too tired to go looking for someplace else to sleep. She showered in the bathroom, blinking at the glare of a single bare bulb bouncing off the white-tiled walls, grumbling to herself about the condition of the shower head. It too needed to be replaced. It was so old nothing more than a rusty trickle of water emerged and it took too long to rinse the soap off her body. When she went for groceries, she'd add a shower head to her list.

She placed a fresh gauze bandage over the incision and pulled on the nightgown she'd bought upon leaving the hospital. Another few days and she'd be able to dispense with the dressings. The incision was still pink, raw-shiny-looking but healed. She wondered—as she had since the operation—if she'd been told the truth or if, in fact, they'd taken other parts of her away along with the cyst. It worried her, the idea that vital sections of her interior might have been removed without her knowledge or consent.

Her stay in the hospital had been a strange, dislocated time. She'd been forced by the lack of anything else to do to consider where she was going and what she hoped for. Her thoughts had turned from the old pattern of considering what she wanted to deciding what she needed. What she wanted was simple enough: to stay alive and enjoy being alive. What she needed was shelter and some sort of income.

Well, she thought, climbing into the creaky bed, now I've got both. Not the best, but not the worst either, and if I stay, I'll fix up these rooms. At least something's settled and I'm off the highway.

The next morning, having set breakfast out on the sideboard on warming trays, she began her attack on the kitchen while father and son in grouchy silence helped themselves to food. With an old dishtowel wrapped around her head to protect her hair and a past-it pair of rubber gloves she'd found under the sink, she was well into cleaning the oven when Cameron walked in to announce, "I'll be going in to my office this morning. What sort of mattress do you prefer? Firm, medium or soft?"

"Medium," she said, glancing over at him. "Thank you."

"Anything else?"

"Where do you usually shop for your groceries?"

"There's an outdoor stall a mile up the road for vegetables. And a supermarket, a not too bad one, about a mile beyond that. Take a right when you come out at the main road and just go straight. You can't miss either one. Tell Mitch at the vegetable stand you're working for me. He bills us monthly. You'll need some housekeeping money," he said, extracting his wallet and laying several bills down on the counter. "Please hang on to the register tapes. Otherwise, buy what's needed. If you run short, I'll reimburse you. Will you need an advance?"

"No, no. Thank you. What sort of beans are they, after all?" she asked, realizing he'd failed to tell her.

"Coffee." He laughed. "Coffee beans. Have a good day. Don't try to do it all in one go, and don't let the old man con you. If he tries to pull anything that strikes you funny, check with me at the office. I'll leave my card here with the money. Good-bye, Margot."

"'Bye," she murmured, watching him go. Hearing him speak her name gave her an odd feeling. The swing-door slowly aligned itself with the doorframe. There was a silence after the front door closed and then the muted roar of an engine starting. She walked to the side window to see him behind the wheel of a new-looking, gunmetal gray Continental. Surprised, she watched the car disappear, raising a cloud of dust in its wake, then returned to the oven. Coffee beans. This was not an impoverished household. Anything but. So how could they live in such filth? Both Cameron and his father appeared immaculately turned-out, well-dressed and clean. Could it be they didn't see the dirt? Or was it just a case, as Cameron had said, of the place getting away from them? Whatever the reasons, there was a challenge here she found she wanted to meet. The concept of turning this house into someplace bright and eminently livable appealed to her. She attacked the stove with a fury.

With that done to her satisfaction, she put the wet laundry into the dryer; started the second load in the washer and began work on the rest of the kitchen. It took her the entire morning to clean the counters, the windows, the Formica backsplash running the length of one wall, and the floor. It wasn't, as she'd thought, light brown, but white. On her hands and knees with steel wool, cleanser, a brush and bucket of water, she went over every inch of it, even digging into recessed places with a small knife.

She then folded the clothes from the dryer while the floor dried, stuffed the second load into the dryer and returned to her hands and knees to wax the floor. Getting to her feet finally, she took the vacuum down to the living room where she planned to begin work after lunch. For half an hour while the wax was drying on the kitchen floor, she enjoyed a cigarette and examined the contents of the living room, looking at the photographs on the mantel, deciding which pieces of furniture were worth keeping and which were fit only for fueling a bonfire. That fire would be a sizable one, she thought, pounding the armchairs and sofa with her fists and sending puffs of dust into the already heavy air. How could they live with this garbage? She couldn't understand it.

She was deep in thought when she heard the tinkling of a bell from above and realized Harley Senior was ringing for her. Like something from a hundred years before. Ringing a bell so she'd come. She didn't like it.

He wanted his lunch.

"You trying to starve me?" he demanded from the depths of the armchair in his bedroom, surrounded by sections of the morning paper. "Where's my lunch?"

"As soon as the floor's dry in the kitchen, I'll make your lunch. But you'll ..."

"... have to come on down to get it," he completed the sentence for her with a derisive smile. "Like giving orders, don't you? I'm the one does the order-giving round here."

He said it lightly, self-mockingly.

"Why do you ring that bell?" she asked. "How would you like someone ringing bells for you? Do you have to do that?"

"How the hell else'm I going to get your attention? You want me shouting down the stairs?"

"I wouldn't mind," she said truthfully. "At least it's human."

"Hate the damned thing myself," he admitted, regarding the small bell with distaste. "Can't remember which one was it started that."

"Well, If you don't like it and I don't like it, let's agree to stop."

"Haven't seen you do any eating yet," he observed. "You found some new secret way of getting nourishment from the air?"

He watched her eyes go distant and saw the fatigue on her pale features and felt guilty for probing.

"What's the matter with you, woman? One minute you're feisty as hell, giving counterorders, and the next minute you're gone all mopy. You running away from home, missy?"

Her eyes connected with his and she bit on her lower lip, trying to decide how to answer that.

"Cam tells me," he went on, "You claim to be thirty-seven." He was eyeing her appraisingly. "You're thirty-seven, I'm King Farouk."

"What do you want for your lunch?" she asked, crossing her arms in front of her. "There isn't much in the kitchen. I'll have to shop this afternoon."

"What is there?" he asked, still studying her.

"I can give you some soup and a tuna salad sandwich. Will that do?"

"I'll let you know after I've had it."

"You know you'll like it," she told him, wanting all at

once to laugh madly. The situation was so absurd. Like a Gothic novel. The runaway wife hiring herself out as a housekeeper to an eccentric old millionaire and his son.

"What's tickling your funny bone, skinny?" he asked, gathering up the sections of the paper.

"You, this house. This house is one jump removed from the Collier brothers! Do you know that? Why don't you *do* something? There's nothing wrong with you. This place needs all the help it can get. It'd be a lot healthier for you to help me than it is sitting around in your pajamas all day letting your body atrophy."

"Well, well! Like what, for example?"

"Like it wouldn't break your arm to lift a dust cloth or push the vacuum cleaner around. If you were interested, maybe we could do something about fixing this place up. You could come shopping with me, show me what food you like. Do you like the way this place is, the way you're living?"

"Like it? Hell! I try not to look at it. What're you up to, lady? Out to rearrange our lives after you've been here one day?"

"Maybe it's what you need. And maybe if we fixed up the downstairs rooms, you wouldn't have to spend all day up here. Don't you get bored?"

"Sit down," he said flapping his hand at her. "Sit down and stop hanging over me like a skinny bird." She sat, instantly feeling the ache in her muscles. She'd never worked so hard in her life and felt she could sleep for weeks, months. "You've got some pretty goddamned high-faluting ideas in your head for somebody hiring herself out to do housekeeping. I'll bet you never did housekeeping in your entire life. Not for pay."

"I did it for free," she said.

"You got a husband somewhere?"

"I grew up with a mother and father. There were things I was expected to do around the house."

"You sure do tell a whole lotta lies," he said cannily. "What's your name again?"

"Margot."

"Margot. You can't come along and change us around just like that 'cause you don't like the way things are."

"What's *your* name? Or do I have to call you mister?"

"Claude. You can call me any goddamned thing you like. I don't care. I been called some hard names in my time."

"I'll bet you have. Anyway, why not?"

"Why not what?" he asked.

"Why can't I come along and change you around? Maybe it's what you need."

"Maybe it's what *you* need," he countered incisively. "You can't just assume people want to be shuffled like a deck of cards. That's pretty goddamned presumptuous. You know that? And how come you never answer questions when somebody asks you?"

"I apologize," she said. "Of course you're right. It's none of my business if you want to spend the rest of your life up here by yourself."

"Don't get all nasty-mouthed on me." He laughed. "Just give me some reasons. Might be I'm interested."

"Really?"

"Well, it isn't all that much goddamned fun sitting around on my keister. That's a fact. But don't you go jumping to conclusions just 'cause somebody likes a little bit of an argument before they go leaping in doing what you want them to do."

All at once, she was aware of and stunned by her behavior in the past twenty-four hours.

"I don't know what I'm doing," she said quietly, as if talking to herself aloud. "I've never acted this way in my life." She shook her head, then stood up and looked around the room, her hands trembling.

"What in hell's the matter with you?" Claude yelled. "You

nuts or something? First you're one thing, then you're another. Sit the hell down and get yourself put together!"

Her eyes moved back to him and abruptly she sat down.

"First one of you damned females to come along here with any halfway decent ideas and before I get chance one to do some worthwhile arguing about it, really sink my teeth into it, you're backing off, wringing your hands."

She didn't hear him. She was thinking, I'm irrational. I must keep quiet. I need this job.

"You're not listening!" he accused, smacking the folded newspaper on the arm of his chair. "Hey! Get your head back down from the clouds and pay attention when somebody's talking to you!"

"Sorry. What?"

He stared at her intently for several moments.

"What're you running from?" he asked softly.

"Nothing." She shook her head.

"Something," he persisted. "Living on nerve. I know it when I see it."

"Don't!" she warned quietly. Their eyes met.

"Go on, get the lunch going," he said at last. "And after that, I'll take a look-see what's what downstairs."

"Will you?"

"Didn't I just say that? Go on! I'm an old man. I need my food. And from the looks of you, it wouldn't hurt you none to do a little eating. Set the table. For two, mind! I'll get cleaned up and we'll eat."

"Yes, sir," she said, getting to her feet.

"Claude, skinny! The name's Claude. You *asked* me, I *told* you. You call me *Claude!*"

"Claude." She smiled. "I like you, Claude."

He flushed. "Go on, get the hell outta here, so I can get dressed!"

✠   ✠   ✠

After lunch, Claude declined her invitation to go shopping with her. She went on her own, returning with a carload of food and cleaning equipment as well as a new shower head for her bathroom. As she was unloading the car via the kitchen door she heard the vacuum cleaner running and after she'd set the last of the bags down on the counter, she walked quietly to the front of the house to see Claude haphazardly steering the vacuum cleaner around the living room, whistling; an apron tied around his waist. She returned to the kitchen smiling and started putting the groceries away.

Once she joined him in the living room, he began a running monologue of complaint but was obviously enjoying himself. Over dinner that night—breasts of chicken, wild rice, endive salad—he told Cameron, "Skinny goddamned woman's worn me out! Imagine forcing an old man to put on an apron and clean house!"

"First work you've done in years." Cameron smiled at Margot. "Won't hurt you."

"Fat lot you care!" Claude accused. "You're just waiting for me to drop dead so you can get the rest of my money!"

"That's right," Cameron said, still smiling. "That's what I'm waiting for."

Margot nibbled at her food, listening, watching them.

"And you shut up!" Claude yelled at her.

She smiled and took another bite of chicken.

"Ever meet such a contrary woman?" Claude went on, his eyes on her although he directed the question to his son. "One minute she's zipping around here dishing out orders like chipped beef on toast. Next thing anybody knows, she's off in dreamland, way the hell out in the clouds."

"Leave Margot alone," Cameron said calmly. "She's doing a fine job."

They're talking about me as if I'm not here, she thought.

"*I'm* doing a good job," Claude argued. "Who in hell you

think cleaned that fucking—excuse me, skinny—stinking living room anyhow?"

"What does it matter?" Cameron asked, again looking at Margot. "So long as it's done." He set down his fork and lifted his glass. "This is superb, Margot. You're definitely the best we've had."

"It's a conspiracy!" Claude forged ahead. "The two of you're trying to kill an old man, work me to death."

"It'd take a firing squad at least forty rounds to kill you," Cameron said, refusing to relinquish his hold on Margot's eyes. "Ignore everything he says. He's in love with the sound of his own voice."

She wished he'd stop looking at her. Wished she could look away. But his eyes held her.

"Smartass!" Claude mumbled, helping himself to seconds. "Goddamned smartass kids! No respect for old folks. Without us, you know, none of you smartass kids'd be here!"

"That's true," Margot said. "Thank you very much, Claude."

"What in hell's *that* mean?" Claude wanted to know.

"I thought you wanted to be thanked for putting us all here."

"Shut the hell up! How can a person eat with you yammering away at him?"

"Sorry," she said. "I forget sometimes how sensitive you are."

"Damned right!" Claude snapped.

Cameron smiled into his wine glass. From one day to the next, the entire tone of their lives had changed. Margot. The old man was crazy about her. I, he thought, could be crazy about you too. But the apprehension he saw in her eyes every time he looked at or spoke to her kept him at a safe distance. She's not afraid of Dad or of making changes, but she's afraid of me. He wondered why, when he couldn't think of anything he'd done that might've upset her. She puzzled him. Yet so long as things continued to go on as they'd started, he'd be perfectly happy.

✠   ✠   ✠

After a decent shower that night, she lay in bed in the dark, listening to the sound of Cameron's footsteps moving overhead. It sounded as if he was pacing the floor. Then the pacing stopped and the house was silent. She folded her arms under her head and stared at the ceiling. What a strange, ugly man, she thought. Then decided, No. He isn't ugly. He really isn't. And being good-natured is being good-natured, not strange. He doesn't do "routines." Except for that bean business. And that really was very funny. Coffee beans. She smiled and turned over on her side. Very funny. Really.

On the third day, her new bed arrived. Cameron had Mitch from the vegetable stand come with his truck and take the old bed to the dump.

On the fourth day, she completed cleaning the downstairs and moved her equipment upstairs to the third floor. She began with Cameron's bare-desked "office" and did the three unoccupied bedrooms up there, as well as the two bathrooms.

On the fifth day, she attacked the second floor, where the three of them had their rooms. Claude, having taken two days in which to recover from his exertions, helped her, constantly grumbling. Every so often, she looked over and smiled. She thought he looked sweet with his bow-tie, his apron, his happily malcontented expression.

On the sixth day, she sat down after lunch and wrote a long letter to her mother and father, giving them the address but warning them to be careful not to leave this or any of her future letters lying about in case Paul came around looking. She told them about her hospital stay and about Claude and Cameron. She told them she was happy. It was true.

On the seventh day, Cameron said, "I assumed you knew. You have Sundays and Thursday afternoons off."

She thanked him. "Would it be all right if I took off today instead? There are some things I need. I thought I'd drive into the city to do some shopping."

"Sure. In fact, I'm going in to the office today. I'll be happy to give you a ride."

"No, thank you. I think I'd prefer to go on my own. I'm not exactly sure where I'm going to have to go to find the things I want. I'm not very familiar with the city."

"Whatever you like," he said equably.

"But I'll be back in time to prepare dinner," she added.

"Take as long as you like. Your off-time's your own. We'll pick up for ourselves." He smiled and watched her eyes go traveling. He had the distinct feeling she didn't listen so much to his words as to the tone of his voice.

"Yes," she said distractedly, planning to go first to a pawn shop. Then, depending upon how much she'd get for the jewelry, she'd be able to buy some clothes, especially under-wear. And, after that, she'd come straight back. It was risky going to the city. Paul might have people out looking for her. She'd come directly back. Where it was safe.

Thirteen

The LETTER FROM HER MOTHER, WHEN IT CAME, brought reality crowding in on her. She sat down at the kitchen table, lit a cigarette and nervously slit the envelope. The letter contained some of what she'd expected: news of Paul's outraged searching for her. "The man is completely insane," her mother wrote. "He insisted we were hiding you somewhere in the house and threatened to go away and come back with the police to search the house. Of course he went away and no police came." She went on to tell of Paul's constant telephone calls, threats, his repeated middle-of-the-night visits to the house when he "… came pounding at the door, shouting your name, convinced you were inside. The police had to come twice. The neighbors telephoned them both times. And on the second occasion, the neighbors pressed charges and he was arrested for disturbing the peace. Also the judge issued a restraining order to keep him away from here. But we are positive he will keep coming back."

Again Margot felt ashamed. Her parents were now witnessing first-hand the irrational, violent behavior of this man she'd lived with. Now they *knew*. And she was certain they had to wonder about the condition of *her* brain. Only someone equally crazy would stay on with a man like Paul. However, her mother went on to say, "It is such a great relief for us to know you are well away and that you have found a position. When you write again you must tell us more about these people you work for and what you are doing." They both sent her love and assured her she was not to worry. They were more than capable of contending with Paul and glad to do so on her behalf. "He is," her mother concluded, "far worse than we ever dreamed. And we blame ourselves for doing nothing to help you. But as long as you are safely away now that is all that matters."

She read the letter a second time, then folded it into her pocket.

The letter did upset her, and that night she had nightmares about Paul. Replays of actual incidents and manufactured ones, terrifying encounters generated by memories. All she managed to repress in her waking hours brought itself to her sleep and took over.

Cameron, having spent two hours doing paperwork in his office, finally returned the papers to his briefcase and pushed his chair back from the desk with a sigh, lighting a fresh cigarette. He sat smoking, listening to the night sounds inside and outside the house, thinking; becoming aware of an eerie noise emanating from the floor below. Holding very still, he strained to hear, to determine the nature of the sound. As he listened, the noise gained in intensity and he realized it was coming from Margot's bedroom.

He crushed out his cigarette, got up, switched off the light in the office and descended the stairs to stand outside her door listening. It was an indescribable sound, a tortured sort of moaning cry. He knocked quietly at the door, getting no response. The cries continued and he knocked again, unsure what to do. He stood for a minute or two with his hand on the doorknob trying to decide. Then, concerned for her, he tried the door and it opened under his hand. The room was dark. His heart thudding, his palms damp, he stepped inside, trying to see in the darkness. The cries coming from the bedroom beyond made his scalp prickle and tighten and he called her name softly, sure she must be having a nightmare. But if he tried to rouse her, his voice, his figure in a dark room would frighten her. He switched on the light then, riveted to the sight of her contorted, sleeping features and the tangled splash of her hair, touched her arm and whispered her name.

She awoke with a jolt and a cry, her eyes flying open. She saw him and, like a wild animal he thought, leaped away from his hand, cringing against the wall, her mouth open with shock.

"You were crying out," he explained, embarrassed. "I thought I'd see if you were all right. I'm awfully sorry for scaring you."

Her eyes remained very round for several seconds, staring at him as if he was someone she'd never seen before. Then she blinked and said, "I'm all right," in a thick, sleep-clogged voice. "You didn't frighten me," she lied. Her heart felt as if it might explode out of her body. "I'm very sorry I disturbed you."

"You're all right?" he asked, looking unconvinced, noticing the slick-looking film of perspiration coating her face.

"Fine. I'm fine. Just a bad dream."

"Well," he said uncertainly, backing up a step. "If you're sure. I'll say good night."

"Yes, thank you."

Her eyes followed his every move as he made his way to the door.

"You'll be all right now?" he asked again. Despite her assurances, she was watching him as if in fear for her life.

"Fine. Thank you. Good night."

"Good night," he said, and closed the door.

She stared at the door for at least a minute after he'd

gone, her arms trembling. Then she looked down at herself. Her nightgown was hanging down over her arms, her
breasts exposed. With a cry, she yanked the gown back
over her, then bolted out of bed, locked the door and hurried back to bed, dropping down against the pillows, sinking her teeth into her fist to keep from crying out again.
She lay for a long time waiting for her panic to subside.

He brushed his teeth thinking about what had happened.
She'd been terrified of him. Nothing like it had ever happened to him before. He'd had women ignore him disdain-
fully, finding him ugly. He'd had women set out purpose-
fully to seduce him, lured by his money. He'd had women
meet him on open ground, prepared to accept him as a
human being. But he'd never had a woman cringe and
cower at the sight of him. His reactions were complicated,
multiple, hard to define. And something else. Something
he'd held away from himself until this minute. Her body.
Her breasts. He'd undressed and made love to women of
thirty-five or older. Margot's was a younger woman's body.
A much younger woman's body. And he'd have held her
gladly, willingly; he'd have comforted her had she not
demonstrated such obvious fear of him. She had seemed
wild to him with her long tangled hair and naked breasts,
her round terrorized eyes. Wild. With fear.

✠   ✠   ✠

"I'm sorry about last night," she said, when he came in to
get his morning coffee.

Disconcerted, he said, "Oh, that's all right," took his coffee and returned to the dining room.

She was positive he'd fire her. He was positive she'd quit.

From the dining room, Claude yelled, "Get your skinny
ass out here and eat a decent meal for a change!"

She pushed through the swing door to see that he'd

heaped food on a plate and set it down at her place.

"I can't eat all that," she began.

"Reason you have nightmares," he said with an ace-up-the-sleeve smile, "is 'cause your brain ain't got nothing to feed itself on. Put a little something in there," he pointed at the region of her stomach, "and you'll sleep just fine. Sure do make one hell of a lot of noise for a scrawny female."

She turned scarlet, convinced he'd next make some remark about Cameron's being in her room. She looked across at Cameron who was reading the morning paper, steadily eating. Please, she prayed, help me out of this! He lifted his head, looked at her and smiled reassuringly.

"See that!" Claude stated. "Cam agrees!"

She let out her breath and picked up her fork. It was going to be all right. Thank you, she said silently. Thank you for not making me suffer.

After breakfast, Cameron left for the city and Claude trailed around after Margot, making garrulous asides as he swung his feather duster here and there—his contribution to the cleanup—noticing that she seemed, since breakfast, to be shedding years right before his eyes. Her eyes were losing some of their wary intensity and her body seemed to be dancing as she efficiently remade the beds, whipped towels off the racks in the bathrooms and laid out fresh ones. Anxious to keep her in this frame of mind, he said casually, "What good's a living room, if nobody can live in it?"

"No good at all that I can see," she answered.

"We don't even have a goddamned working TV set."

"Why not?"

"I can do any damned thing I want!" he declared as if she'd challenged him.

"Of course," she said, scouring the sink.

"Don't talk down to me, skinny! I'm not so far gone I

don't recognize condescension when I see it."

"I wasn't condescending." She rinsed the sink and turned to sprinkle cleansing powder in the tub, then got down on her knees and scrubbed it around.

"You like cleaning up, don't you?" Claude asked.

"I don't mind."

"You like it here, eh?"

Her head turned and she regarded him carefully, smiling. "I like it here."

"Let's go buy us a great big color TV," Claude suggested. "I like those old movies, you know. And it's about time we got another set."

"What happened to the one you had?"

"Wore out. Cam said he was tired of spending money fixing it. So Mitch took it off to the dump in his truck."

"I see." She stood up and turned on the faucets to rinse out the tub. She had a dull ache at the base of her spine. All that bleeding after the operation.

"Tell you what else I wouldn't mind having," Claude kept on, sitting on the toilet seat watching her.

"What's that?" she asked, sloshing the last of the water down the drain, thinking she'd have to make a trip to the drugstore in the shopping center, wishing she could be finished with the bulky sanitary pads. But the doctor had told her not to use tampons until her next period.

"What're you talking to me for if you're not going to listen?"

"I'm listening," she said, wondering yet again if the bleeding was supposed to be going on this long.

"I said I'd like to go have a look round that furniture place up Route 27. You know the one?"

"I don't think so."

"Where you from anyhow?" he asked. "You sure as hell don't come from anywhere around here."

"Back East," she said vaguely. "You're not thinking of buying new furniture, are you?"

"I might be. It'd make it a whole hell of a lot easier cleaning up in there if we got Mitch to come on down with the pickup and haul that load of moldy crap off to the dump. Rugs 'n all. Get all that stuff outta there, we could maybe do up the room real nice."

She smiled at him.

"Hate that shit-eating grin of yours!" he said, pleased by her reaction.

"What about Cameron?" she asked.

"This is my place, case you're interested. Mine. Cam's got his own wherewithal. But it's me who pays you, skinny. So if I want to go buying things, I'll go buy 'em. And don't you forget it!"

"I won't. Are you serious?"

"God*damn*! What about?"

"Doing over the living room."

"You got any taste to speak of?" he asked tartly.

"It's *your* house. Shouldn't you decide what you want?" She collected up the soiled towels and her cleaning gear and moved to go.

"Hey, skinny?" he said quietly.

"Yes?"

"Nobody else ever seemed all that interested before. You know?"

"I know," she said softly. "I think it'd be really nice to be able to sit together in the evenings."

"You're an all-right kid, skinny. Just don't go thinking I'm soft in the head. Just 'cause I'm old doesn't mean I'm sappy. I know what's what."

"You're not that old."

"Sixty-eight," he said proudly. "Not bad for sixty-eight, huh?"

"I think you're terrific. Let me just change my clothes and we'll go shopping. Okay?"

"Well, hurry up!" He grinned.

✠   ✠   ✠

It occurred to her while watching Claude examine various television sets that she felt about him in a way she'd never felt about anyone else. They shouted at each other, they argued. They exercised their sarcasm, they were snide. But there was a boundary, a line beyond which neither of them would go. To cross that line into the territory of intended injury, malicious backbiting and words like poison meant to kill, would mean they'd stopped respecting each other; ceased caring. She cared, each day, more, for this aging man; more than she had for anyone but her mother and father. She'd never known her mother's parents. Her father's parents were people she'd seen only twice—they'd lived too far away, in Quebec. Claude was like a grandfather, a friend, a companion. They were never bored in each other's company, and their sarcastic wordplay seemed to invariably move them into some sort of productive action. Like now. Claude was haggling over prices with the salesman and she stood, enjoying him.

"Come on," Claude said, marching over to her.

"Did you get one?"

"'Course I got one! Isn't that what we came for? It's going to be delivered tomorrow afternoon, along with the antenna. Naturally"—he shot an accusatory glance backward at the salesman,—"we've gotta pay an extra how-d'you-do to have the antenna put up on the roof. Crooks. They're all crooks, these fellas. Like used-car dealers. Never met a one of those who could look a person straight in the eye. All of them trying to pass off somebody else's headaches."

As they were heading toward the furniture store he'd told her about, he asked, "How come you got such a fancy car, a housekeeper?"

"I earned it," she said, noticing new growth on the trees, a few brave daffodils showing their faces. "How do people get things?"

"That's plain stupid, skinny!" He sounded annoyed. "Most people got what they've got without doing one damned thing except asking. Don't you know any better than that? There ain't all that many people willing to do some hard work for what they want. Like most of you women. You just latch on to some hard-working rube and tell him what you want, expecting him to go out and get it for you. You think it's your privilege to make demands, what you get for letting him marry you in the first place."

She looked across. He was serious.

"Well, aren't you gonna argue with me about that?"

"I'm thinking," she answered. "I'm not sure you're not right in some ways."

"That right?" He smiled and laid his arm across the back of the seat looking very pleased with himself. "I'm not so stupid."

"You're not at all stupid. Maybe it's what I thought," she said, half to herself; questioning her motives, her expectations of the marriage.

"How's that?"

"Nothing. Is that the place?"

He swallowed the remark he'd been about to make and impatiently waved his hand in the air in front of him. "Park over there," he instructed her. "And don't you go trying to talk me into buying a whole houseful of fancy furniture. I'm buying what I want, not what you want."

He stalked the sofas and armchairs, the coffee tables and lamps with an expression on his face like that of someone attempting to determine which beast was most likely to attack him.

"There's too goddamned much stuff in here," he complained, unable to make a decision. "What d'you think of this here thing?" He indicated a black naugahyde sofa that would have looked perfectly at home in a dentist's waiting room.

"Awfully hot to sit on that in the summer," she said carefully. "Something lighter in color would probably be more comfortable."

"That's what I thought," he said, scowling at the black sofa on his way down the line of sofas before coming to a halt in front of a floral-printed loveseat. "What about this?"

"You're giving my powers of diplomacy a real run for your money." She smiled. "Why don't we try to work this out together? There's really a nice one over here. Come tell me what you think of this."

A long, low-slung Lawson sofa upholstered in sturdy, bright green fabric.

Claude sat down and bounced up and down several times, then ran his hand along the arm of the sofa before looking up at her skeptically.

"It's a hundred less than that black one. And comfortable, too. Right?"

"It's not bad," he said offhandedly. "I suppose I'll have to get a couple of fancy chairs to go along with it."

She could tell he liked the piece and was having a great time as he picked out two armchairs that went surprisingly well with the sofa. Highly pleased with his success and well into a mood for spending, he hurried her along to the rug department to select a shag carpet in green and white, holding it by the corner, turning to her to ask, "This one?"

"It's perfect. Beautiful. You have good taste, Claude."

"Don't you con me, skinny!"

"Honestly, it's beautiful. And think about this: If we haul everything out of the living room and paint the walls white—strip off all that ugly old wallpaper—and maybe paint the moldings and trim this same shade of green, can't you just see what a lovely room it would be?"

"All right, all right," he agreed, seeing it.

As they were driving back to the house, Claude had her stop at the shopping center where they bought paint and brushes, rollers and scrapers.

"God*damn*!" he exclaimed, slamming shut the trunk of the car. "I can't wait to get shut of all that moth-eaten crap of Elsa's. Been sick of that furniture since the day she picked it out. Soon's we get back, let's get started stripping that wallpaper. We can have that room ready'n waiting for the new stuff if we get at it now."

"Claude, are you sure you're not trying to do too much in one day?" she asked gently.

"There you go again! Changing horses! Why do you *do* that, woman? It's goddamned infuriating! You know that? Can't you stick with something once you make up your mind?"

"I was thinking of you ..."

"The hell you were! I'll tell you what *I* think: I think you're scared me or Cam we'll change our minds and blame it all on you. You're scared of Cam and don't deny it! How in hell can you be scared of someone as easygoing and harmless as Cam? Or me for that matter? Something about us that bothers you?"

"Of course not."

"God, how you lie, skinny! You're about the lyingest woman I've ever met. I'll be damned if I'll keep on asking questions when it's plain as day you're not about to give out any answers. But it seems to me the least you could do is keep your mind to the track once you've decided on some-thing. Some folks would be pretty upset having you around changing your mind every ten minutes, you know."

"I won't do it again," she said, seeing herself from his van-tage point and understanding he was right. "If I do do it again, be sure to remind me."

"And one other thing," he continued, determined to get

some truthful answers out of her if it was the last thing he ever did, "how come you arrived here smelling like a hospital? Where'd you come here from?"

"The hospital," she answered truthfully.

"What kind of hospital?"

She laughed. "You think I escaped from a mental institution, don't you, Claude? You think I'm a loony on the loose and there are all kinds of people in white suits running around looking for me."

"Well," he said, "are you?"

"Of course! Why else would I want to live with a crazy old man like you?" She laughed again, then started the car. "I had pneumonia," she said, glancing into the rearview mirror. "And some surgery. *Not*," she appended, "on my brain. Now stop prying! I'm not telling you anything else today."

✠   ✠   ✠

They pushed everything into the middle of the room and while Claude covered the few good pieces with old sheets before going off to change into some work clothes, she readied a casserole for dinner, humming happily to herself.

By six-thirty, when Cameron arrived home, they'd stripped one wall and were at work on the second. Cameron stepped into the living room doorway, staring at the two of them—plaster-dusty and surrounded by torn strips of wallpaper.

"What's going on?" he asked, as their two smiling faces turned towards him.

Margot's smile collapsed. She read the look on Cameron's face and knew there was going to be trouble. And trouble came with irrational accusations, blows to the body.

"Could I talk to you privately, Margot?" Cameron asked.

She set down her scraper and followed him out to the kitchen.

Fourteen

CAMERON WAS SO PERPLEXED BY THE DISPLAY OF DREAD and fear on her face it took him several moments to marshal his thoughts. It was the second time she'd been this way with him—like a cornered animal—and part of him wanted to shout at her to stop it. The other part of him wanted to take hold of her—as one would a small child— and physically soothe her, stroke her calm. Her fear of him had the effect of making him feel uglier and bigger than he was. As if he'd been transformed into something inhuman and grotesque and she was breathlessly waiting for him to demonstrate the totality of this transformation by unsheathing his claws, baring his fangs.

"Why do you look at me that way?" he asked at last.

"What way? I'm sorry."

It was automatic, he realized. She wasn't even aware of what she was doing.

"Never mind," he said. "Do you mind if I ask what's going on around here?"

"Your father ... liked the idea of doing over the living room. I thought ... I thought it would be good for him to get actively ... involved."

"And just how involved is he?"

"New furniture ... a television set." Her eyes were round, fixed on him. Her body seemed tensed for flight, her hands coiled at her sides.

"New furniture and a television set," he repeated. "Why?"

"Why? Because they're needed," she said softly, waiting for him to begin spewing out aberrant arguments. "The living room goes unused. The furniture you have is falling apart. And a television set ... he wanted one."

"No, no," he said patiently. "Why are *you* doing this? Is it some sort of game you think you're playing with my father?"

"Game? I don't understand."

"There have been a few other women who came here thinking they'd ingratiate themselves, possibly set themselves up for some sort of inheritance."

"My God!" she said, appalled. "You must have a low opinion of me, Mr. Harley. I'd *never* do a thing like that. I care very much for your fa ... I ... if that's your feeling about me, I think it would be best for everyone if I leave."

"Slow down. Take it easy," he said calmly, holding up his hand. "I'm not accusing you of anything. I just asked a question. Maybe I'm a little too blunt. I've been told that I am sometimes. I'm just trying to find out if you're really aware of what you're doing, if you realize you're building up his hopes, building up his dependency upon you."

"Is that wrong?" she asked, becoming angry. "He's a lovable human being. He has a right to involve himself. It's his home, isn't it?"

"Of course it is. You're making this sound like a personal attack on you, making me sound like some kind of monster, that I resent my father's feelings for other people."

"Don't you two talk about me like I'm not here and don't have perfectly good ears to hear with!" Claude said loudly from the doorway, brandishing his scraper. "What's itching your ass, Cameron?"

"I was simply asking Margot to explain to me what's going on around here. I go to work in the morning and when I come home I find the whole place turned upside down and the two of you tearing apart the living room. I'd just like to know what's going on and why."

"That's pretty goddamn obvious, I'd say," Claude said coolly, crossing the room to stand beside Margot. "Skinny here and me, we bought some new stuff for the place. About time, too. Then in you come with your eyebrows all up in the air, saying a lot of nasty goddamn things. She was a man, she'd be in her rights to haul off and wallop you one, Cam. Where d'you get off accusing her—or anyone—of plotting against me? That makes me pretty goddamn mad, that. As if I ain't got brains in my head but sawdust and you're the only one around here who can do any kind of straight thinking. You don't think I can tell the difference between somebody who's plain interested and somebody's got ulterior motives? I've got a college education, too, you know. You went too far, Cam. Too goddamned far. Half the time you come over plainly indifferent, just smiling away as if you don't give one good goddamn. The other half of the time you're busy looking for conniving meanings to the well-intentioned things people like to do. You can't be indifferent and involved, too, you know. And it pisses hell outta me you drag Margot here out to make an argument with her as if I'm halfway to the grave already and not worth talking to!"

"I think I'd better go ..." Margot started.

"And what in hell's the matter with you?" Claude demanded. "First feel of heat you're going to get outta the kitchen? Don't be such a fucking coward! You stay right here and defend yourself, goddamnit! Don't you go running off now, making me look bad; making me look a fool for listening to someone won't even stand up for her opinions!"

"I think if she wants to go you should let her," Cameron said quietly, at once realizing his words would be misunderstood.

"She doesn't *want* to go!" Claude shouted. "Speak up, woman! Tell him so! Don't go dumb! Speak up!"

Both men looked at her expectantly.

"Since your father was willing ... interested in making some changes ... I can't see any reason why he shouldn't."

"Damn right!" Claude said, egging her on.

"But I won't put myself between the two of you. I'm an employee. It's not ... to create problems. I ... *This place is disgusting!*" she cried out, feeling herself being forced—as with Paul—into an arbitrarily defensive position. "Maybe *you* don't care about it," she accused Cameron, "but your father does. And ... me ... so do I. I thought it would be ... nicer, more like a home people live in ... I ... I don't need anybody's *money*." She was going to cry and struggled to hold it in, feeling deeply hurt by the accusation he seemed to have been making. "I'd never *dream*," her voice was cracking, "I wouldn't try ... to ingratiate myself ... not with anyone to cash in on ... a death. That's terrible ... a terrible thing to say to me."

"But I didn't say you were," Cameron argued. "I didn't *say* any of that. This is getting way out of hand."

"Goddamned right!" Claude said, warming to the argument. It was the first time in years he'd seen Cameron lose his perennial smiling calm.

"I just wanted an explanation," Cameron said, flustered. "I do apologize if I've offended you," he said to Margot. "It wasn't what I meant. I only wanted to know what was going on. That's all."

"Hurty feelings," Claude taunted his son.

"Don't *do* that!" Margot snapped spontaneously at Claude. "It's my fault," she addressed Cameron. "I misunderstood what you were trying to say. But it isn't easy to know exactly what my position here is supposed to be. I may not have done this particular job before, but I do know what I'm doing in this house goes a long way beyond 'housekeeping.' I hope you can see that."

"Perhaps," Cameron said cautiously, "you've taken on a little more than the prescribed duties."

"If I have, it's because there are things around here that need doing badly. And I care. About doing the job I'm paid to do. And ... the people who pay me to do it." Suddenly, she didn't feel angry or defensive, but simply positive. Very, very positive. Cameron was looking at her in a way he never had before—as if he was actually seeing her. Or perhaps it was the first time she'd revealed herself to these people. His eyes were assessing—or reassessing her—and unafraid, she fixed her eyes on his until he looked away, over at his father.

"Are you planning to continue working after dinner?" Cameron asked them both.

"'Course we are!" Claude answered. "How the hell else we gonna get that stinking room ready for when the new stuff comes? Goddamnit! The TV's coming tomorrow. We only got two more days after that and I'm not putting brand new furniture into that room looking the way it does!"

"Perhaps," Cameron said, "I'll lend a hand then."

"Is this 'discussion' over now?" she asked softly. "I'd like to get dinner on the table."

"It's over!" Claude said, hurrying off to wash up before dinner.

Cameron continued to stand beside the counter after his father had gone. He watched Margot adjust the thermostat on the oven and check the casserole. Finally, he said, "I am sorry. I wasn't accusing you of anything."

"I realize that," she said, pulling vegetables out of the crisper, not daring to reveal her eyes to him.

He placed his hand lightly on her arm and she jumped away from him, making a small, startled sound that she attempted to stifle with her hand. His eyes wide, he withdrew his hand as if he'd burned himself on her skin.

"I'm sorry," he said.

"No," she said, quaking inside. "*I'm* sorry." She took a deep breath and unclenched her fists. "I think that evens things out."

He looked confused.

"It isn't you," she said. "I'm the one with suspicions about people's motives. Not you."

They stood looking at each other. The kitchen clock ticked off the seconds. He had questions he wanted to ask, words he wanted to say.

"I'm in a really difficult position here," he said at last.

She understood at once what he meant and felt heat rushing into her face.

"This isn't something that's happened to me before," he continued, fearing that if he didn't explain himself now, the opportunity would be lost forever. He had to get the words out while she was holding still. "You don't ... You're not like anyone else we've ever had here. And I ... can't seem to get myself to think of you ... that way."

"I see," she said almost inaudibly. "Maybe it would be best if I went."

"That's not why I'm saying this," he said quickly. "Not to point out the negative side of things. How do you feel?"

"I *can't!*" she said, wishing this wasn't happening. Yet she'd known since the night he'd awakened her from her nightmare that this would happen. "I think I'm going to have to explain. Later? Could we talk later?"

"You don't owe me any explanations."

"I think I do. Under the circumstances."

He hadn't been wrong. There was something happening. And he was all at once tremendously optimistic. Whatever problems existed could be solved. Everything could be solved. She wasn't telling him no. She was telling him she'd explain. It was funny, he thought. Until minutes before, he hadn't known how he felt. He knew now.

"We'll talk later," he said.

✠   ✠   ✠

The three of them worked in relative silence until almost ten when Claude tossed down his scraper, saying, "That's it for me! You two would work an old man to death. I'm going up to bed."

They said good night and listened to Claude's footsteps ascending the stairs. Margot felt her heart constrict apprehensively; her palms damp as she set down her scraper. She was alone with this man. Alone. He was a man. She was so aware of him she felt she was suffocating.

"How about some coffee?" Cameron proposed, pushing long strips of wallpaper into the trash barrel they'd brought in from the garage.

"All right. I'll put on the pot."

"I thought we could go out for some. The diner on 27 stays open all night."

"I'll tidy up and get my jacket."

I'm going to have to tell him, she thought as she washed her hands at the kitchen sink, then untied her apron. I'm going to tell him because I *want* to tell him. And I don't know *why* I want to tell him. I *do* know why. My own reactions scare me now. All of them. Because I don't really believe it's safe. There are no guarantees that a man who'll treat me gently at the beginning won't beat me later on. Still, I can't live forever without some kind of contact. And he seems so reasonable. None of the things I thought mattered when I started with Paul matter now. All I want or need for my future is peace, a peaceful life. That's all. To be needed, valued, to belong. To be treated respectfully. To have my needs, desires handled as if they're of importance—simply because they're mine.

I knew it that night I told myself he wasn't ugly. I didn't

find him ugly. I could see how other women might. But I couldn't. I'm not twenty-one anymore and I don't look through the same eyes I had then. Or perhaps I *do* look now. I can see more clearly. But still with fear. I'm so tired of being afraid, wish I could stop fearing, but how? Perhaps by starting with the truth.

Sitting on opposite sides in the booth at the diner with thick white mugs of coffee untouched before them, she began trying to explain. To both of them. It was the first time she'd attempted to put words to the thoughts and feelings. She'd written about all of it in her letters home to her parents but she'd never voiced her continuing reactions.

"Your father likes to accuse me of being a liar," she said, gazing down at the steaming coffee. "He's right. I am. I've lied about almost everything I've told you." She raised her eyes to see she had his complete attention and, at once, lowered her eyes again.

"I have a husband," she hurried on. "I had to get away from him. If I hadn't, he would have killed me. I've never talked about it. Not even to my parents ... when it was happening. They knew. They couldn't help but know because Paul took the evidence and pushed it in their faces. It was as if he was saying, 'This is what I can do! Look at her! Do you see my power?' I thought then he'd be ashamed. Something. But he wasn't rational enough to see his actions in anyone else's light. He saw them as justified. And I went along, playing my own game of justification. Because being beaten, abused was too humiliating, too shameful. I couldn't merely accept that. So I had to rationalize, say it was because he was this or that. The truth was he was sick.

"It wasn't just Paul. It's hard to explain. It wasn't only him. It was the town, the people who lived there, the things that went on. What was happening with Paul and me, that was bad, terrible. But when I began to see that the whole ... society around us was sick, I had to run. I didn't want to lose myself, lose the things I thought I believed in. I'm saying this badly.

"I used to be someone—before my marriage—who'd hear about women whose husbands beat them and I'd say, 'Not me! The first time any man hit me would be the last time he saw me.' But he hit me and he cried and because I believed I cared for him, I had to try to understand why he'd done it. I knew he'd been abused as a child. He told me about it. I latched onto that and used it to death as justification for everything that happened afterward.

"The people all around us ... the things that were going on ... there was a parallel. The only people I knew who seemed to have definite values, realistic wants and emotions were my mother and father. I knew when I first became involved with Paul—it was too fast, too easy and I knew it then but wouldn't admit it, not to anyone—that my parents wouldn't be able to help me. I was making the decision, or allowing the decision to be made for me, whatever, and there was nothing anyone could do for me. So, finally, it was up to me to, decide.

"For six years I refused to face what was true, what was real. I believed—I wanted to believe—I could make him change, I could make him see what he was doing, make him stop. I couldn't. The only one I could change was me. And if I stayed, the only change I'd have made was from living to dead. Several things happened. I left everything and ran for my life. One of the ... things ... that happened ... there was a woman. She died. I tried to save her. I thought I could. She died. And then I knew, *really* knew there was no one to save *me*. Only me. I had to save me. So I ran. And ran." She stopped and cleared her throat before continuing. "I got ... sick. Double pneumonia and some ... internal problems. And wound up in the hospital in the city here. When I got out all my money was gone. I didn't have any choice. I had to take the job you were offering. I'm not sorry I did." She looked up at him again. "I don't want *you* to be sorry that I did."

"And how old are you really?" Cameron asked quietly, trying to absorb the images she painted for him.

"Almost twenty-eight."

"Why did you lie about that?"

"I honestly don't know. Protection, I think. I think I thought if I told you I was older I might be left alone. Or respected. Something. I'm not sure what I thought. I was so tired. And in shock. Running. I needed the job."

"Does anyone know where you are?"

"My parents. I've written to them. I am sorry," she said sadly. "I didn't start out intending to tell a lot of lies. It just felt so ... necessary."

"You have a way of making yourself sound like a criminal," he said judiciously. "I can't see that you've done anything that's so wrong."

"You can't?"

"Not really," he said, turning his cup around so that the handle was pointing toward her. "It sounds as if you've had a pretty rough time. I guess it's understandable you'd tell a few lies. It's not that hard to understand really."

"Have you ever hit a woman, Cameron?"

He examined her eyes. Thinking, You want to be convinced about me. It's not my way—selling people, convincing. I don't know how to do that for you. Except with the truth, perhaps.

"Once," he admitted. "I did once. In the army. I guess there's nothing in my life I'm more ashamed of than that. I hit her just as hard as I would've hit any man. Knocked her cold. Then I stood there, shaking like a leaf, astonished at what I'd done. It happened right in the middle of a lot of action. The tension was bad, *bad*. Nerves. She was a nurse. I'd slept with her several times. And she wanted to get at me for some reason, trying to rile me. I was young, scared. I hit her.

"It was all part of that war thing, I think. The doubt most of us felt, wondering what we were doing in Korea when the war was supposed to be over. I hated myself for acting so … primitive. You have to ask yourself why you do the things you do and if you've got any sort of personal integrity, you can't be too proud of doing something like that. It doesn't *prove* anything, I don't think. Except that you're bigger and stronger. It's not hard to be a bully, a tough-guy, if you're not thinking. It's the only time I've ever hit *anyone*. But I did do it."

While he was relating this incident, she felt herself beginning to trust him. She believed him. And the thought came to her that belief is the basis of trust. Being able to trust, I might begin to care. I want to care, she thought, surprised. There are so many things about you I like.

"Have you been married?" she asked, picking up her coffee cup.

He nodded and followed suit, picking up his cup. "When I was too young again," he said, his eyes focused on some vague spot just past her right ear. "After I got back from Korea. It was all over within a year and we got divorced. Twenty-seven," he said, his eyes moving back to her. "You're even younger than I'd thought."

She shook her head. "It depends on the kind of wars you've been in. I'm never going to be young again. How old are you?"

"Thirty-eight."

"You're younger than *I* thought." She smiled and finally drank some of the coffee.

"What will you do now, Margot?"

"Do? Nothing. Stay here, try to forget it happened. No, not forget. Remember it. Maybe one day use it somehow. I'm not sure. It's still too new. And it's still not over. Not in my head."

"The nightmares," he said.

"That. And other things. Things I'm not ready to talk about yet."

He knew what things. Knew without having to be told. And knew why she cringed and jumped away from him when he'd tried to touch her.

"It wasn't you," she said, as if she'd read his thoughts. "I didn't know I'd react that way. It made me feel awful, seeing myself do it. But I can't help myself. I think," she said thoughtfully, "my experiences with Paul have somehow programmed me. I keep expecting to be hit. I also think I was trying, without realizing it, to provoke you in that direction tonight. I was misunderstanding you on purpose, I think. To see if you'd behave like Paul."

"My dad's crazy about you," he said. "You've done wonders with him, revived him."

"I think he's reviving me. I hope you're not really upset about the redecorating. It's not because I wanted to interfere or exercise my powers of persuasion or anything like that. It's just that it seems so wrong to let a beautiful old house go to ruin. And it's just as wrong to waste a beautiful old man. We all need to feel important, that we're needed."

"That's true."

"And we recognize each other," she said. "We know one another."

"He's a proud, stubborn man. He'd never admit to needing help. Not after my mother died. He tried to keep up the house on his own with a local cleaning lady who came in one day a week. But when he had the coronary, something had to be done. So I moved back, hired a housekeeper. It needed doing. I can't truthfully say I don't miss my privacy, my own place, my own life. Not to mention the inconvenience of living this far from town. I miss the night life, the shows. But I guess it all boils down to sentiment. I love him. I've seen it happen too many times where feelings went unspoken and then all of a sudden it was too late. Somebody died. And there were no chances left for saying, I love you. I'd rather be with him now, having him know that I care. My life'll still be here later on."

"Someday," she said, "I'd like you to meet my mother and father. I think you'd like them. I think they'd like you."

"Someday," he said incisively, "you're going to have to do something about Paul. It'll reach a point where you'll want to know where you stand."

"You're right. I know that. But I'm not ready yet. I don't know when I will be ready. Just thinking about him, I get the feeling I haven't run far enough. I'm afraid he'll turn up on the doorstep one day."

"Is that a possibility?"

"I don't know. Anything's a possibility." Caring for you, she thought. That's a possibility.

✠   ✠   ✠

On the way back to the house, secure, almost cozy within the confines of the luxurious Continental, Cameron looked over at her to say, "I hope you do understand what I was trying to say earlier. About your motives and my father. I didn't mean to come across vicious. I just wanted to know what was happening. You were right about that, you see. You're not the typical housekeeper. And maybe I felt a little jealous about the results you were getting with my dad. We all have our childish moments."

"I know. I'm glad we've talked."

As they were walking from the garage to the house, he stopped her, taking hold of her arm.

"There's something I'd like to do," he said very softly. "Trust me. Don't fly away."

He lifted her chin and kissed her lightly on the mouth, then released her. She stared at him throughout, then hurried on ahead of him into the house. She was drenched with perspiration, her heartbeat rapid. For the duration of that quiet kiss, she'd been unreasonably, insanely terrified.

As she raced up the stairs to her room she was furious with herself, despairing of ever again being able to respond purely, openly to displays of affection. She silently cursed Paul for what he'd done. He'd harmed far more than her body. Until Cameron kissed her, she'd been unaware of the extent of the damage. Now awareness had been forced upon her and with it a new fear: that she'd never again respond.

Fifteen

THEY DISCUSSED IT, AND THE LIVING ROOM RE-DECO-rating project became the whole house re-decorating proj-ect. Once the living room was completed, its fresh white walls and green trim, the bright new furniture made every other room look even dingier, dirtier. So they moved the dining table and chairs to one side, covered those and the sideboard—all fine pieces of furniture that required noth-ing more than a good cleaning and polishing—and painstakingly set to work stripping the dismal coach-and-four-horses wallpaper from the walls. A coat of yellow paint on the upper walls and ceilings, the waist-high paneling stripped, refinished and polished, the floor sand-ed and waxed and the dining room became warm, inviting, aglow with welcome.

At mealtimes, they debated the question of Which Room Next? It had become like a game, redoing the house. Since they were doing the work themselves, including floor sand-ing—Cameron was very pleased at being able to master the awkward, rented machine—the cost per room was mini-mal. Paint, polish, wood-stripper, wax and the price of the fabric Margot sewed into curtains on the old treadle sewing machine that was unearthed from the garage. The spacious downstairs rooms were cheery, homelike. Now that they were done, the attack was moved to the long main-floor hallway and foyer. The ancient, disintegrating runner was discarded and the three of them selected and purchased a new one, then returned home to stand staring at the scarred, scratched floor shaking their heads in dismay.

"We'll have to rent this sander by the month instead of by the day," Cameron said with a laugh. "I guess we might as well get started. If the need for coffee beans ever runs out, I'll be able to hire myself out doing peoples' floors."

While the polyurethane finish was drying on the front half of the hallway, they used the rear staircase that ran upstairs from the kitchen. And while the rear half was drying, they used the main staircase, posting signs to keep themselves alerted.

During these working hours, Margot or Cameron hurried out to pick up food at the all-night diner on 27 or at the delicatessen in the shopping center. They sat around the kitchen table eating hungrily, commenting on their progress, admiring their efforts.

It took close to a year to get all the rooms done over.

On the third floor, they changed one of the unused bedrooms into a sewing room. Cameron arrived home beaming, carrying a new portable sewing machine which he presented to her, watching with pleasure her delighted response. They knocked down the flimsily constructed partition separating Cameron's office from the second unused bedroom and made of the two a comfortable, decent-sized retreat-office. With new curtains and slipcovers Margot found to her pleasure she was able to create from patterns, the third and final unused bedroom was made over into a guest room.

On the second floor, more floor-sanding was done, more painting, polishing and waxing, more curtains and slipcovers made. But when it came to Margot's rooms, she asked, "Would it be all right if I did these over on my own time?"

"'Course it's all right," Claude said. "I've had it with

working. It's about time I got a chance to enjoy the TV without having to jump up every ten seconds 'cause one or the other of you two wants to come roaring through with some machine."

His eye was caught by the overgrown garden and soon he was outdoors cutting back the bushes, pruning, clipping, promising next year in early spring he'd do some serious work outdoors.

Cameron walked through the house with a look of pleased disbelief, touring the rooms again and again to admire what had been done. He was amazed at what they'd accomplished. Amazed every time he looked at Margot.

In the course of the year she'd gradually lost her gaunt, haggard look, becoming rounder, younger looking, more ready to laugh. Her eyes still frequently retreated into dark, secret regions but for the most part now flashed with inter-est and a quiet kind of excitement. She seemed always to be moving; stirring something on the stove while she read a book propped against a pot on the counter; flying out to her car to drive to the market or the hardware store. The elderly, yellowing plastic-housed radio that had sat idle on the kitchen counter for years played classical music by the hour. She seemed to be moving to the music as she swept through the house, the thick plaited rope of her blond hair bouncing against her spine as she went.

He watched, almost seeing her gathering strength, grow-ing. He'd come into the kitchen for a cup of coffee to find her sitting at the table writing page after page of yet anoth-er letter home. The letters from her parents arrived regu-larly each week and she hurried upstairs to her rooms to read them with both eagerness and apprehension.

Cameron continued his social and business life in the city, dating often; occasionally awakening at one or two a.m. in the bed of a woman friend to bestow hasty farewell kisses as he somewhat guiltily hurried home. Having

Margot in the house was in many ways like having a wife. He deplored the idea of her discovering his empty bed some morning. So he struggled into his clothes and made the hour's drive back to the country over the truck-filled throughway.

In the course of the year, something upsetting began to occur in the midst of his lovemaking activities with one or another of his female friends. He'd suddenly think of Margot and find himself growing harder, becoming gentler, even more attentive than usual. The result of this was a deepening attachment to him on the part of two of these women. These attachments both mystified and alarmed him because they weren't what he wanted. He wanted things to remain fairly much as they were: Margot and his father waiting for him at home.

It was a gradual process, this growth of dependency, and he was only partially conscious of it. It simply happened that with each month's passing he became more and more accustomed to the new warmth of the house and the presence in it of two people he loved.

Often, coming upon Margot unaware, he'd stop and feel himself filling with affectionate concern for her, with further questions he wanted to ask but felt required an appropriate opening. So, along with the dependency there was growing a fear that she'd one day recover herself so totally she'd no longer require a hiding place and she'd take herself back to where she'd come from. He found he could scarcely bear to contemplate her leaving. The idea of it made him become tense and despondent, as if he were, in advance, enduring her loss. The longer she stayed, the deeper the despondency became when he considered her eventual departure. He didn't know what he'd do, had no idea how he'd cope in that eventuality. It brought him so low he tried not to think about it.

On half a dozen occasions, having worked well into the

evening on one or another of the rooms, the two of them went out to the diner for coffee and conversation; to sit quietly talking through the steam of the coffee and the smoke of their cigarettes. At those times, he felt an encompassing pride and pleasure in being seen with her, in having the counter-man and the waitress greet them with recognition. As if they were two people together and the outside world understood that.

Twice, upon returning home, he kissed her; each time a little more disappointed when she flinched, then stared at him somewhat breathlessly for several seconds before rushing away. He was, at the end of that first year, at a point where he often lay awake at night trying to will away the fairly painful evidence of his need for her.

He had dreams that she came to him in the night and slid her body over his, opening her thighs in monumental silence to take him inside herself. He awakened from these dreams with what felt like an ache in his arms from having striven so hard to contain her within them. He fled from these dreams directly to the arms of one or the other of his two women friends.

✠   ✠   ✠

After the first few months, her mother wrote that Paul had ceased his nocturnal visits and intimidating telephone calls. The silence thereafter was ominous. Margot felt it through her mother's words, felt it inside herself as her eyes raked the city streets during her visits to town. As long as Paul had been actively engaged in seeking her out, she'd felt somehow secure in the knowledge of his whereabouts. But now he might be somewhere nearby. He might be watching the house or following her, might have hired detectives who'd managed to trace her and were keeping track of her comings and goings on his behalf. And the car, even with re-registered plates, was still recognizable, trace-able. Simple really to check with the Department of Motor Vehicles and find that Margot Seaton Rayburn had taken out a local driver's license and registered the car. She was convinced if he ever did find her it would be because of the Buick.

Still, as time passed and nothing happened, she began to relax. Her appetite returned. And after five months of her fearful waiting and worrying that something had gone seri-ously wrong inside her, her periods started again. She greet-ed the return of her blood-flow almost joyfully, grateful to be able to finally use the tampons she'd been keeping in her dresser drawer. Ceremoniously, she bathed herself, then inserted the tampon, surprised to find that the act of inser-tion was oddly pleasurable. It was the first time, since Paul, that anything had entered her body. She became once more aware of her sexuality, of the appetites that had all but died away.

Along with renewed awareness of her body came a heightened awareness of Cameron. He was available and she was in need. In the nighttime stillness of her room she visualized his making love to her and became aroused, liq-uid. Yet when he was in the same room with her she felt herself involuntarily shrinking away from him, shying beyond his touching range. When he bestowed occasional chaste kisses upon her closed lips—having successfully managed to keep her still long enough to do so—she want-ed with everything inside her to return those kisses, enlarge them. But her arms refused to surround him, her body remained stiffly distant. She couldn't do it. Her mind held an image of a beating. It wasn't Paul wielding the belt, but Cameron. No matter how often she told herself Cameron seemed congenitally incapable of such an act, she couldn't take herself past the image. To be beaten again, to be vio-lated, would mean the end. Of her. Of her life. She couldn't go through that again. It had taken almost all of her strength to escape the first time. She doubted she'd survive a second.

So she studied him when he wasn't aware of her, noticing the soft depth of his eyes, the breadth of his back, the swell of his genitals against his trousers. She looked at his hands, his ears, his neck, the way his hair fell over his forehead and his casual habit of pushing it away. The sound of his voice penetrated the cavities of her body, buzzing inside her like small drills working away at her pressure points.

She observed his patience and kindness with his father. He was unfailingly kind, consistently kind, astonishingly kind. He swallowed Claude's sarcastic comments and asides with a good-natured resiliency and humor she admired and envied. Cameron was, she knew absolutely, the kindest man she'd ever known. But knowing it failed to convince that doubtful segment of her brain that insisted it was merely a ploy, that he was capable at any moment of becoming violent. He never would, she told herself. Never. Still her eyes, her brain remained vigilantly watchful, suspicious, reserved.

Claude took tremendous pride and pleasure in the results of their efforts. He sat in the living room in the evenings watching television, contentedly chomping the stem of his pipe—even lighting it some evenings—expansively congratulating all of them on a well-done job.

"Come the spring," he said, "we'll get started outdoors. Whole lot of work needed out there. Know anything about gardens, skinny?"

"My father is a great gardener. I have a lot of trouble telling the weeds from the flowers. Sometimes the weeds are prettier than the flowers."

"Goddamnit! I knew it! I'll have to do the whole goddamned thing myself."

"Of course you won't," she said placidly. "You'll just have

to teach me which are weeds. And we can plant new bulbs and seeds."

"More money, naturally! How come everything you do costs me money, woman?"

"It was your idea." She smiled.

"I didn't say word one about any new plantings."

"Oh! Well, then we won't."

He was about to comment when she flashed a brilliant smile at him. Caught, he smiled back, saying, "Up the volume on that box, will you? I can't hear what those idiots are saying."

The evenings when Cameron was at home were like festive occasions. They dined ceremoniously in the dining room, then moved to the living room for coffee. In the winter, with a good fire going in the fireplace, they'd sit quietly, all three of them peacefully absorbing the quality of this life they'd established together. Serenity was invading her through her pores and she opened herself to it gladly, relishing these moments; storing them away as if there might come a cold, empty season when she'd have great need of them.

She'd look up from the needlepoint she was teaching herself with the aid of an illustrated book and gaze at Claude, then at his son, reminding herself this was an illusion, impermanent. One day, she'd have to leave here and all the feeling would be lost. She never wanted to lose it, never wanted to leave. At these moments, she wished decisions never had to be made, that life could be ever changing yet static. Impossible, she'd think, and return to the pattern she was creating on the canvas.

On those evenings when Cameron stayed in the city, she and Claude ate together in the kitchen. Afterward, they'd play gin rummy or checkers and she'd try not to speculate on what Cameron might be doing at any given moment. She knew he was seeing women, dating. And heard him

tiptoe into the house at two or three in the morning—
sometimes as late as five—with a knot of jealousy in her
throat that threatened to choke her. But she told herself
she had no right to be jealous of his outside affiliations.
Especially since she seemed to be completely incapable of
offering him any alternative attentions. She wanted, wanted, needed. But her misgivings held her firmly locked in.

As the pressure of her conflicting emotions built, she took
to self-gratification on those nights when Cameron stayed
out. Behind her locked bedroom door, having showered,
powdered and perfumed herself, she attempted to ease the
accumulating hunger. She'd study the scar on her belly and
wonder if she might now be considered disfigured. It worried her. She tried not to think about it. And it required
very little effort to send her into relief-giving convulsions
that allowed her to plunge into sleep like a corpse being
tossed into inky waters from a bridge in the dead of night.

✠   ✠   ✠

In the second year, she joined the local library and actively resumed her reading. She also fell into the habit of going
once a week with Claude to see a movie. On his birthday,
Cameron took them out for an expensive dinner. It was an
evening filled with laughter and Claude's biting but enor-
mously pleased remarks, and the three of them returned
home happily sated and sleepy.

She didn't feel lonely, had no desire for friends outside
the house; she was content to linger over cookbooks of a
morning while the dryer leaked the satisfying scent of
freshly laundered linens into the kitchen and the smell of
yeast tingled in her nostrils. She'd taught herself to make
bread. And gradually, she stopped smoking. She'd never
enjoyed it, had only picked up her first cigarette as some
sort of feeble, self-defensive measure. So now she stopped

and felt air return to her lungs and the taste of food return to her mouth. Her body was strong, healthy again and she studied it at times, trying to come to terms with its independent demands for attention. There were all sorts of things she could change: her attitudes, her hopes and expectations, her habits. But she couldn't control her body's growing craving for the weight of another body, the gentle message of hands not her own, the incoming surge of flesh within flesh. At the most unexpected moments, she would feel the moist heat of longing dampen her upper thighs and she'd glance around wondering if Cameron or his father could sense or even possibly smell her lust. Color would leap upward from her neck into her face and ears and she'd busy herself with some trumped-up or genuine activity in order not to give herself away. She was slowly, slowly melting inside and if she wasn't terribly careful, the process might turn visible, and these two men would witness her turning to butter on their kitchen floor.

Cameron would sometimes turn to find her eyes on him, a stricken expression creasing her face. He'd start to move toward her only to have her blink several times rapidly and then look away. Constantly he found himself chewing up words along with the dinners she prepared. He wanted to speak but felt the weight of impossibility in the situation, so gave up. And, without fail, spent the next night ardently transferring his affections to some other woman.

Exercising tremendous self-control and a forced awareness of the fine quality of her life here, she drifted through the second year and into the beginning of the third. But she had to know. There were too many questions requiring answers. And her curiosity and fear about Paul's lengthy silence became too much to contend with.

"I have to know what's happened," she confided at last to Cameron one evening over coffee at the diner. "I can't stand it any more, not knowing, hanging suspended in a kind of frightened limbo. I'm just not sure how to go about finding out."

"I've got a friend, a lawyer. Maybe he'll know how to do it. Would that be all right with you?"

Grateful, she said, "I'd appreciate it very much. You're very kind about all my … You're kind."

"Let me work on it," he said, looking discomfited by her words of praise, of gratitude. That wasn't what he wanted. But he didn't dare express what he truly, deeply desired. He couldn't risk scaring her away. He also felt he couldn't cope with the flinching response he was sure to get.

He wanted. What I want, he thought. I want to take your hand, hold it; kiss the back of your hand, both hands, have them meet my hands, have our fingers meet, close together, linked. What I want is to follow the line of your shoulders to your throat, go from your throat down, take it down, take you down, hold you gently down, bring you with me down, know the shape of you, the feel of you, want you to want me to lay you down.

Sixteen

IT SEEMED ALMOST TOO EASY, SHE THOUGHT. WITHIN three weeks, Cameron telephoned her from his office in the city to say, "Hal checked the filings and found out Paul divorced you close to a year ago. For desertion. Hal's sending for a copy of the papers."

She was confounded, unable to believe it. Woodenly, she thanked Cameron, then replaced the telephone to collapse heavily onto one of the kitchen chairs, gulping down air as if she'd faint. She was free, had been for nearly a year. A year she might have spent very differently had she known.

Over. Paul was gone from her life, no longer someone she had to fear. She wasn't sure she should allow herself to react, wasn't sure it could all be so easy. But Cameron had told the truth. And had sounded plainly disappointed when she'd expressed no desire to discuss the news he'd just given her. She was afraid to talk about it with Cameron. They both knew now there was no valid obstacle remaining between them. Rather than feeling relieved, she felt more frightened than ever. Not of Paul anymore. Of Cameron, his knowledge of the details of her life, of her deepening attachment to him. She'd been safe up to this point, protected by legalities. Suddenly she was free and faced not only with the right to move about without fear, but faced as well with the daily sight and sound of

Cameron.

Desperately anxious to communicate her feelings, her relief and sudden dreadful confusion, she reached for paper to write her mother.

Ingrid wrote back at once expressing her own relief and two clippings. One showed Paul in a studio-portrait photograph beneath which was the announcement of his promotion to senior vice president of his company. An engulfing spasm of revulsion shook her when she looked at his face and promptly, without thought, she set fire to the clipping, dropping it into the ashtray to watch it burn. The act was another purification rite. When the paper had been reduced to filmy black ash, she crushed it, grinding it down to a smeary residue with her thumb before picking up the ashtray and washing it carefully at the sink. Then she sat down again and picked up the second clipping. A five-line announcement of Paul's remarriage to Melinda Sue Downing.

God help you, Melinda Sue! she thought, resisting a sudden temptation to pick up the telephone and warn Melinda Sue of the experiences she'd just signed on for. But no. I'm free. It's over. I can take my own future anywhere I choose, do with it whatever I fancy.

She wished the options had never been presented to her, that she'd never allowed her curiosity to force her into finding out because her freedom was only external. There was nowhere she wanted to go. The only people she longed to see, besides Claude and Cameron, were her mother and father. Yet the idea of climbing into her car or boarding a plane to go to them further frightened her. If she returned, she risked encountering Paul. So it wasn't over. Married, not married, the fear flourished. Fear, she discovered, required far more than legalities to dissolve it. It had its own set of rules and formalities, and she hadn't any idea how to remove herself from it.

She attempted to explain her dilemma in her letters to her parents. As always, her mother's answering letters—usually footnoted by her father—were encouraging and realistic. "Take your time. You're still young. We're going to be here. All will be well. In time."

Cameron watched her, waiting to see if she'd suddenly become altered or if she'd go away. But nothing changed. Everything went on as before except that she seemed too often preoccupied, slightly dazed. As if the news he'd delivered hadn't been good but catastrophically bad. He didn't understand her reactions but waited, as always, for her to volunteer her thoughts.

Claude wondered if Cameron wasn't going to go to his grave a victim of his own indifference. Or was it indifference? He was damned if he could figure out either what was going on inside his son's head or in Margot's. He'd look over the top of his newspaper in the evening to see Cameron's eyes on Margot. He'd wait, hoping something would be done or said. When nothing happened, Claude closed his teeth over the stem of his pipe, deciding it was none of his goddamned business so he'd keep his trap shut.

Thinking their separate thoughts, each of them contented in their ways with different aspects of their lives together, they traveled forward into spring. The outside of the house was repainted by Mitch's two sons, and, side by side, on their knees, Margot and Claude spent the early spring weeks pulling weeds from the flower beds, then worked at planting new bulbs.

"I think a coat of whitewash on these rocks here would do nicely," Claude said, standing back to study the rock-line perimeters of the two large flower beds.

"A coat of whitewash would do nicely on most things," she observed philosophically.

"That's a hell of a rotten philosophy to have at your age," he said. "You think that's true?"

"No," she admitted seriously, studying his face in the unforgiving glare of the midday sun. "I don't think so."

"You planning to spend the rest of your life here?" he asked atypically, having given up asking direct personal questions some time back.

"I hadn't thought about it," she lied. "I don't know. Maybe. There are worse places, worse people."

"True enough. All kinds of them," he agreed. "You're driving my son half out of his mind. I suppose you know that."

She flushed and looked down at the ground.

"Well," he persisted, "do you *know* that?"

"I know," she said hoarsely.

"What're you planning to do about it?"

"Nothing. I'm not planning anything."

"Look me in the eye, skinny! Come on, look at me here!"

She lifted her head and looked at him

"Okay," he said, his eyes boring into hers. "Now keep on looking at me, hear! It's an old man's prerogative to speak his mind. So I'm speaking it. I don't know what you're afraid of and I don't much care what you're afraid of that's gone before. But I'll tell you this: I know my son. And much as I hate to be admitting it out loud to anybody, he's a fine, decent man. You were the one who said it, you could do a whole hell of a lot worse."

"I know that."

"He's in love with you. D'you know that too?"

She nodded.

"And what're you?" he asked. "What're you, Margot?"

"Afraid," she whispered. "I'm afraid."

"Well, you listen here to me," he said, taking hold of her hand, "listen. You're too young to go through the rest of your life being afraid. It's none of my business, I know that. But you're … important to me. So I'm telling you, it's not the way. Don't throw your life away being afraid, skinny.

You won't get one goddamned worthwhile thing accomplished that way. Not one thing! That's all I'm going to say." He let go of her hand and looked at the rocks. "I guess we might as well get going on these. Why don't you hop into your fancy machine there and go get us some paint?"

She closed her eyes and let her head rest on his shoulder, breathing in the smell of his pipe tobacco and the aroma of freshly turned soil clinging to his hands as his arm went around her.

"Go on," he said, easing her away. "Get the paint. It's starting to cloud over. I'd like to get the first coat drying before the rain comes."

She got up and walked across the lawn on unsteady legs, slid behind the wheel of her car and drove to the hardware store in the shopping center. She felt dizzy, disturbed and moved mechanically, setting the two gallon cans of paint in the trunk of the car, then climbing back in behind the wheel to drive back to the house.

He wasn't in the garden. She went in through the front door to see him asleep in his favorite chair in the living room. Smiling, she crossed the room preparing a witty remark when she felt the unnatural stillness of the room. And of Claude. Before she was halfway across the room she knew he was dead. She continued forward, feeling the stillness penetrating her.

So quickly—had he had some warning?—he'd gone away. She stood beside the chair for several moments, then knelt and pressed his cooling hand to her cheek, keeping it there for a long time as a voice in her head softly sighed, Oh, Claude, I'm sad to see you go.

Yet there was, within those minutes while she sustained her second exposure to death, an understanding of the rightness of this death. The richness of it pervaded her senses. And she was awed by its perfection, could see it only in the light of a reward for a lifetime's striving toward any number of goals; the ultimate, most meaningful being death itself.

In her previous thoughts about death and considerations of her own, perilously close confrontations with it because of Paul, she'd been fearful; greedily, tenaciously clinging to the life she had determined should run its proper course. But this death contained aspects of serenity, of so fitting a close to life's struggles that she was temporarily unable to grieve or even to cry. She simply wished to remain close to this truth, to this man who'd managed without undue pain or lengthy suffering to slip from one state of being to another. Because Claude wasn't dead. He'd gone, she felt, somewhere else; leaving behind the skin sheath that had enclosed him.

That was something else she'd never considered: that her body was merely the housing for her soul, or whatever it was the essence of her self was called. A temporary shelter she might provide for a child, should she bear one.

Even if she no longer believed in heaven and hell and those other indeterminate places where souls were said to collect, she had no doubt at all that Claude had managed to cross from one life into another, perhaps less encumbered one. He no longer had need of the body that had contained him. Excess baggage, he'd surrendered it. She experienced an encompassing gladness at how neatly, how splendidly, nature and Claude had achieved this transfer.

After a time, she got to her feet and went out to the kitchen to telephone Cameron at his office.

The instant he heard her voice, the way she spoke his name, he knew. And, unprepared, the blow fell to his solar plexus, robbing him of air to breathe and words to speak.

"I can't talk now," he said in a voice neither of them could recognize. "I'll be home."

He hung up and laid his head down on his arms, dry-eyed. The tears were there but he couldn't shed them. He pushed

211 CHARLOTTE VALE ALLEN ✠

himself upright, switched off the desk lamp and left.

It was Cameron's immediate and audible response that brought grief to her, erasing that almost euphoric state of wonder she'd been caught up in. She turned slowly from the counter, all at once overwhelmed by the emptiness of the house, her mouth opening to cry out, "*Claude!*" in a voice so shattered and plaintive it sounded as if she fully intended to summon him back to his body before he traveled too far away.

"*Claude!*" she cried, disbelieving now, feeling she'd be drowned by the wave of love and grief that rushed up into her throat and sprang from her eyes. "Claude." She leaned against the wall and wept as she never had in her life, so lonely for him that her body felt emptied, her spirit bruised. That natty, snappy, spirited man would never again bellow her name down the stairwell, summoning her toward some new adventure. "I loved you," she cried, distraught, turning round and round, scanning the empty air.

She picked up the telephone and called her mother to spill out her sadness in fragmented sentences and incoherent, hiccough-punctuated cries. Her mother listened, expressed sympathy, then said, "If you wish to come home now, come. It's been a long time. And we miss you."

"I can't think. I'll phone you again when I can think, decide."

The call eased her somewhat, enabling her to pull the scattered parts of herself back into one while she waited for Cameron to arrive.

✠   ✠   ✠

Pale, his mouth a tight line, Cameron spent several minutes alone in the living room with Claude before going upstairs to his office to begin telephoning. Margot prepared coffee, took it up to him on a tray, then descended once more to the kitchen to start dinner. She didn't know what else to do and feared if she didn't keep moving, go on performing, she'd come apart altogether and perhaps never successfully retrieve all the pieces.

Two men from the undertaking establishment came to take Claude away. As Margot listened from the kitchen, Cameron told them, "He is not to be embalmed, made-up, or put through any of that. I want a plain pine coffin. Sealed. And arrange for a cremation the day after tomorrow. It's what he wanted."

Listening to him giving orders to the two men, she realized she wanted to see him show some outward sign of his grief and realized, too, that he wouldn't. He'd retain his control, force himself to contain his grief until he was alone. She sensed this was what he'd do and found she wanted to take his grief upon herself, share it, enter it. She wanted them to see this through together.

He returned upstairs to make still more telephone calls, finally appearing in the kitchen almost two hours later looking disoriented, exhausted. Like an automaton, he slumped into the chair beside the table and stared off into space for quite some time before speaking.

"There'll be a handful of locals, you and me," he said at last.

"I see," she said dully.

He said nothing further and fumbled in his jacket pocket for cigarettes, lit one and stared into the smoke without blinking.

Uncertain of what to say or do, she worked around him, laying two place settings at the table, bringing over the food. When she'd finished, he looked up at her blankly. She put food on his plate, then on her own before sitting down opposite him. Neither of them moved to touch the food. They sat looking away from each other, without appetite. She wondered why she'd worked so diligently producing a meal she'd known would never be eaten. It was all part of a continuing effort she'd been making to avoid facing certain of her feelings that she saw now were inescapable.

For months, years, this man and his father had provided her with food, shelter, money and, more importantly, respect, tolerance and love. She'd taken all of it, attempting to reciprocate by giving what she could: her attention, her labor, her limited emotions. She couldn't help feeling now that she'd reaped far more in reward than her efforts warranted. The time had come, was here, when she might demonstrate the depth of her feelings by stepping outside herself, going beyond the leaden gates of her fear to make a gesture. Not only from gratitude and sorrow, but from love. Because she'd loved the father and she loved the son. She wanted to. But she couldn't.

Finally, without a word, she got up and left the room.

She lay throughout the night wishing he'd open the bedroom door and come to her, knowing he never would. She had, with all her disclosures, her confidences, barricaded the way. He would never cross the hall and come to her. If it was to happen, it would be up to her to take the first steps.

God! she thought, help me, I can't. I know I swore I'd never ask for anything ever again. But I'm asking again now. Not for myself. For him. Please let me get past this.

She fell asleep at last—near three-thirty—and arose the next morning feeling in no way changed or strengthened. The day was intersected by telephone calls, all of which Cameron took upstairs in his office. She brought his lunch up on a tray and took it away uneaten two hours later. They didn't speak. He didn't even look at her. She sat for hours at the kitchen table staring at the wall, hating herself for being the coward Claude had accused her of being. Hating herself, unable to break out of the prison the fear had constructed.

Seventeen

ALL THROUGH THE BRIEF CEREMONY AND THE FUNERAL itself, her eyes were fixed on Cameron, for the first time noticing the streaks of gray in his hair, the deepening creases at the corners of his eyes. She wondered how much time did she think she had that she could allow it to continue to flow an unimpeded course without attempting to take that time to herself and shape it, use it? Not enough time, she realized. Never enough.

She wished—in vain, she knew—Cameron had never been privy to the secrets of her life, the reasons for her flight. Had she never told him, never made him her confidant, her present problem wouldn't exist. He would, in all likelihood, have instinctively turned to her for comfort, for solace. And she, in all likelihood, would have sought to give these things.

Claude's body was taken away in its unadorned, simple box to be burned and she heard him cautioning her against fear. How do I stop? she asked herself, asked her memory— or the spirit—of Claude? You left without telling me that.

The remainder of the afternoon was taken up with serving refreshments to the unexpectedly large number of people who'd turned up both for the service and at the house afterward. Claude's friends. People who'd loved him, who'd seen beyond the sarcastic displays to the man beneath.

They came, openly admiring the house, eating food they brought with them and drinks Cameron offered, chatting easily to each other and attempting to speak to Cameron who couldn't speak, could only listen, not hearing.

After everyone had gone, Margot moved through the living room and dining room collecting up plates, emptying ashtrays, carrying leftovers out to the kitchen to carefully wrap and refrigerate them. Cameron remained in the living room, smoking one cigarette after another, watching his cigarette smoke rise into the air making random patterns.

With nothing further left to do, Margot went back to the living room, to stand in the doorway looking in at him, feeling herself leaning in toward him, bending toward him. Her throat constricted, her hands damp, all of her wet with fear; she was determined not to succumb to it. Not now. In a voice that seemed to resound with her damnable fear, quivering with it, she spoke his name and he turned, looking at her questioningly.

For a moment, her mouth remained open but nothing would come out. Then, holding herself together, she wet her lips and said, "I'll wait for you." Then she stepped away and went up the stairs.

He continued to sit staring into the space where she'd been not certain he hadn't misconstrued her meaning. Then he got up.

I can't do it, she thought, her limbs stonelike as she switched on the bedside lamp. I can't, she thought, icy-fingered as she stepped out of her black dress and laid it across the chair. I *have* to, she told herself, removing every article of clothing covering her body. I must.

She went into the bathroom feeling sickeningly premeditated as she washed between her legs, then dried herself. My God! she thought, trembling. I feel so strange, so frightened, so unequipped to be doing any of this. The scar. She looked at it, knowing he'd find her disfigured.

She stepped out of the bathroom to see Cameron filling the bedroom doorway.

He waited for her to hide herself, to cry out or demand to know what he thought he was doing. But she did none of those things. She continued to stand where she was, waiting, battling down the panic that turned her entire body to stone now, immobilizing her. She lifted her hand to him—incapable of doing more—and he walked the length of the room like someone sleepwalking, to enfold her in his arms as a cry ripped through his chest and tore from his mouth, as he hid his face in her hair and let the cushion of her body absorb his shock.

After a moment, she reached up and began undressing him. Her mind was filled with visions of torture, with the dread of pain. But she kept on, boldly facing the expanse of his chest as she bared it, risking the damage his body might inflict upon hers as he moved to help her and allowed her to witness his inability to rise beyond his own pain.

She lay down on her bed and he stretched out beside her, his eyes closed, his face wet with tears, his chest shaking.

She looked at him, feeling nothing. Only a need to help him, soothe and ease him. And laid herself on top of him, gently prying his hand away so she could look deep into his eyes before placing her open mouth over his, fitting her tongue against his. His eyes closed once more and he sighed so hard their two bodies shook with the force of it as his hands spread themselves on her back, holding her close.

She couldn't lose herself or her awareness of everything that was happening. His skin was so different from Paul's, the feel of him different. Paul's skin had been hard, textured. Cameron's skin was fluid, softer-feeling. Yet his body wasn't soft. It was firm, broad, muscular. His mouth pleased her. The shape and feel of it, the way he returned her kisses pleased her. But she still felt premeditated, mechanical.

And he remained unaroused between them.

I must, she told herself, disengaging his arms, slipping away to put her hands and then her mouth to him, ignoring all the words and images cavorting around her brain as she caressed him, revived and awakened him, knowing full well his grief had deprived him of any capacity he possessed for active performance. And she was grateful for this. She had to do this herself, complete this gesture, make it totally. And so she attended to him, encouraging him to swell until she'd succeeded in enflaming and arousing a weapon that might prove capable of killing her. Having succeeded this far, she placed her desensitized body upon his and drew him in, noiselessly breaking into tears as he rose up into her, then gathered her down on his chest.

Their faces wet, their mouths joined, they moved together. Without pleasure but with a profound sense of having made a significant step forward, she slid back and forth urging him to come inside of her, to somehow heal both of them in the process. He held her face in the curve of his neck, blindly straining within her body, unable to force it, to keep on. He stopped.

She remained motionless, held captive by his arms, her face in his neck, reading his body through her own, following his descent into quiescence. He remained shrunken, reduced inside her body and she believed she'd failed. She sobbed, ashamed, her eyes shut tight against the horror of this failure.

And then one of his hands came to life and slowly traveled the length of her spine and up again.

"I don't know what to say to you," he murmured. "So many things, thinking all kinds of different things, but I can't find any one thing I want to say first."

He paused, shifted slightly, but remained inside her. Her legs lying either side of him felt inhumanly heavy. She couldn't move, didn't dare to.

"It wasn't the way I'd … imagined it might be," he said. "But maybe this was the only way. I don't know. I can't seem to think." His eyes moved over the room seeing the changes she'd made, taking in the slipcovers and curtains, the softly patterned wallpaper and carefully painted moldings, the new lampshades and pictures she'd placed on the walls. His hold on her tightened slightly and he pressed his lips to her shoulder. He wanted very much to talk to her but couldn't. They'd joined without touching, had started making love without loving. He was slowly returning to reality, aware that he was here in her bed in her room, holding her, and he'd looked at her body without seeing, entered her body without feeling. But the contact had restored his vision, his senses, and now he wanted to look, to see, to touch and feel, to collect the sense and sight and scent of her and impress these things upon his mind.

Wrapping his arms securely around her, he turned, bringing her down under him, all the while maintaining the slight connection.

Please don't, she thought frantically. Don't, I can't, please. But he would, was going to, and her mouth trembled, her eyes scoured the darkened corners of the room searching out a hiding place. There was none. This had been her hiding place. Now, no more. And she'd known all along there was a good chance he'd return to himself and find it necessary to explore the dimensions of this gift she'd attempted so clumsily to offer him. Coldly, clinically, like an internal examination it was necessary to suffer, she'd extended a small portion of herself in the vain hope he wouldn't look for more. She'd failed. In all ways. Now the control was his and he possessed the power, the strength to take what was left of her life and smash it, destroy it.

He lifted himself slightly, allowing his weight to rest on his elbows. His eyes pierced hers until she felt she'd be swallowed up by his eyes and his unasked questions. He'd ask now without words, finding his own answers.

The fear turned her rigid as his eyes began to shift down, taking in her throat, her shoulders, her breasts, arms. And now his hand reached out to contain her breast, to mold itself over her breast, learning the shape and feel of it, its contours. He held her breast, trying to turn it conversational, his fingers shocking her nipple into withered silence. Her belly cringed beneath his hand like an old woman who'd always lived in darkness without ever learning any communicable language. Her thighs remained closed around him like the doors of a crypt. His traveling fingers flicked switches along the length of her body, bringing startled whimpers from her throat, causing her hands to flutter like frightened birds, twittering mutely either side of her head. He placed his lips in the indentation at the base of her throat, stilling her cries; brought his mouth grazing round the circumference of each breast before applying his tongue to her nipples, sending her heart into jungle rhythms pounding out warning messages. His hands stroked the hollows beside her hips and her hands flew to her mouth to lie curled against her exposed teeth like terrorized children trying to hide behind their own shadows. He grew inside her, making a gratified sound as he laid his mouth down on her shoulder, her neck, her ear, as if convinced he could tenderly kiss away the layer of suspicion and icy reluctance hindering access to all her responses. He made statements upon her she was powerless to dismiss and her body lifted itself closer as if to hear more clearly the promises he was making.

Her legs locked tight together, trapped beneath his, she couldn't move. And his body was telling her, Stay, stay! Stay? When Paul had always insisted she coil herself about him like a hypnotized cobra? Stay? But he was growing inside her, taking root inside her, starting to move inside her, creating pleasure inside her. The delicate persistency of his mouth and tongue in her ears, on her temples, her eyes, her mouth was dragging her out of herself, leaving her bare, defenseless. Her hands came away from her mouth and slid down to rest on the sides of his face as she began to become convinced, moaning softly at the receipt of his answers, her entire body riding forward to meet him, her mouth holding his.

He stopped. His mouth left hers and all the blood in her went rushing off to the remotest points of her arms and legs. He stopped and she gazed at him wide-eyed.

"Don't fight me," he whispered.

She shook her head once, slowly, tasting her own tears as she opened her mouth to speak to him. "It's too late," she whispered, bringing him back, bringing him close. "I love you. Too late."

"Too late?"

"Please," she said tremulously, "I don't want you to stop now."

"Do you want this? I can't help feeling this isn't what you want."

"Cameron. Your name is Cameron. I know you. I know I know you. I want …" She wiped her face with both hands, then put her hands to his face. "You. I *want* you."

Down, sink down your broken voice and all the pain I'll bandage you with love anoint you with love ease you down with love. Let me, I'll be a bridge to carry you from everything fearful.

"Never," he whispered. "I'll never hurt you."

"I know you, I know."

He brought his mouth back to hers, tasting the sudden sweetness of her responses; holding her beneath him still, he recommenced his motions, savoring the increasing heat of her body, the swelling of her flesh surrounding him. He felt the excitement building in her, felt joyful in the knowledge that communication was finally taking place.

She let her eyes close, gave up her guarded tensions, letting them slip away, felt his body striking sparks, grew taut as the fire caught, and failed to hear the long, gasping cry that emerged from her throat as she was electrocuted back into life.

"What was this?" he asked, tracing his finger the length of the now-fading scar.

"The surgery. An ovarian cyst."

"And these?" he asked, discovering the faint markings on her breasts and belly.

"Paul's belt."

He kissed each scar, then stroked her face, shaping it beneath his hands, going on to do the same to her breasts, her buttocks and thighs, whispering, "I love you," over and over again, "I love you."

✠   ✠   ✠

They sat side by side at the table eating breakfast and laughter was bubbling up inside her, rising from her belly into her chest, reaching her throat. She clasped his hands and held them with all her might, shaking her head as she tried to fight off the laughter but it wouldn't be stayed. Her mouth opened and it floated out deliriously, enveloping him, causing him to first smile hesitantly, then to grin and, finally, to laugh; their hands linked like the most intricate of Chinese puzzles.

"Oh God!" she said as the laughter ebbed. "Should we be happy now?"

"Yes," he said. "Yes, definitely."

✠   ✠   ✠

They walked through the garden hand in hand, thoughtful. "Cameron," she said after a time, "when I came home and realized what had happened, that he'd died, I have to tell you … I envied him. So much. I wanted that end for myself. To quietly slide away. The rightness of it, the simple rightness. I held his hand and wished it had been me. It seemed so unfair because life—despite all his complaining and arguing—life delighted him, energized him. It didn't seem fair that he should go while I stayed on, doing battle. I was so jealous. Like that day you came home and found us stripping the wallpaper and you were so angry and hurt. Jealous, you said later, calling it a childish moment. This time it was my turn, sitting on my knees holding his hand, half of me in awe at the magnificence of being allowed finally to leave life and the other half of me craving fullness, craving life. I felt as if I was standing halfway across an immense bridge between life and death and no matter what I did I couldn't get to the other side any faster. Like those dreams where your feet turn to cement and you want to run but you can't. You try and try, your whole body straining, your lungs bursting and all you can accomplish is a few inches forward."

"It's better," he said simply, "to live."

✠　　　✠　　　✠

She lay beside him in his bed lazily stroking his chest, awed by the simple fact of his reality.

"What're you thinking?" he asked, soothing out her hair, spreading it in patterns on the pillow.

"I'll get pregnant," she said softly. "I haven't taken my pills for three years."

He raised her chin so she could see the smile breaking his face.

"Good," he said happily. "Good!"

✠　　　✠　　　✠

He pushed the cart up and down the aisles of the supermarket while she selected things from the shelves and set
them down in the cart.

"Do you like these?" she asked, turning, holding out a jar
of artichoke hearts.

"Would you like to go home?" he asked, taking the jar
from her and putting it in the cart.

"Would you come with me?" She stepped closer to him.

"Would you want that?"

"Yes," she said. "I'd want that."

"How," he wondered aloud, "will you introduce me to
them?"

"How?" she repeated. "How? I would say, 'Mother, father,
I want you to meet Cameron, my friend!'"

"And?"

"And my lover."

"And?"

"And what?" she looked puzzled.

"What do you *want* it to be?" he asked seriously.

"What do *you* want it to be, Cameron?"

"Could you include husband in that introduction?"

"Maybe on the next visit?"

"Okay." He smiled. "That's okay." He lifted the jar of artichoke hearts and gave them to her. "Put these back, will
you? I really can't stand them."

She laughed and put them back. They moved on down
the aisle.

✠   ✠   ✠

About the Author

Charlotte Vale Allen was born in Toronto Canada and lived for three years in England before moving to the United States in 1966. After working as a singer and cabaret/review performer, she began writing full-time with the publication of her first novel LOVE LIFE in 1976. The mother of an adult daughter, she has lived in Connecticut since 1970.

✠   ✠   ✠

Get in Touch

If you would like to comment on this book, or you would like to be added to the author's mailing list in order to receive notification of forthcoming books, please write to:

Charlotte Vale Allen
c/o Island Nation Press LLC
144 Rowayton Woods Drive
Norwalk, CT 06854

✠   ✠   ✠

Visit the author's website at:
http://www.charlottevaleallen.com